Tess must choose between running for Miss Coronado and entering the school mural painting contest with Erin. There are big opportunities—and a big blowout with the Coronado Club.

THE SPEAKER SYSTEM CRACKLED TO LIFE. "HELLO? CAN YOU hear me?" the principal shouted into the speaker.

"Yeah, they can hear you in California!" Russell shouted, his hands covering his ears. He flopped on the floor like a landed fish. Tess lifted her head and watched his clowning. So embarrassing. Didn't he have any pride?

"In your seat please," Ms. M. told him, and reluctantly he slid back into his chair.

Principal Twiddle continued, "I'd like to announce the nominees for Mr. and Miss Coronado. Ladies first. For Miss Coronado you've nominated Jillian Benson, Lauren Mayfield, Melody Shirowsky, and Tess Thomas."

Tess shot up in her chair, stunned, and looked around the room. Me? There must be some mistake!

With thanks to the many women and girls who faithfully read these manuscripts, offering both advice and love: Peggy King Anderson, Debbie Austin, Megan Baltierra, Amber Beyer, Linda Campbell, Rachel Gunn, Robin Jones Gunn, Kristy Kirchmeyer, Tricia Kirchmeyer, Heather Marsteller, Stefani Marsteller, Valerie Marsteller, Sara Mike, Jane Orcutt, Sue Overby, Carolyn Ratley, Christine Suguitan, Danica Suguitan.

Secret Sisters: (se'-krit sis'-terz) n. Two friends who choose each other to be everything a real sister should be: loyal and loving. They share with and help each other no matter what!

War Paint

Sandra Byrd

WaterBrook
PRESS
Colorado Springs

War Paint

Published by WaterBrook Press

5446 North Academy Boulevard, Suite 200

Colorado Springs, Colorado 80918

A division of Bantam Doubleday Dell Publishing Group, Inc.

Scriptures in the Secret Sisters series are quoted from the
International Children's Bible, New Century Version,
copyright © 1986, 1988 by Word Publishing,
Dallas, Texas 75039. Used by permission.

The characters and events in this book are fictional,
and any resemblance to actual persons or events
is coincidental.

ISBN 1-57856-020-9

Printed in the United States of America

1998—First Edition

10 9 8 7 6 5 4 3 2 1

one

Declaration of War

Monday, February 3

"Okay, I've been waiting all day! Tell me your great plan." Tess Thomas sat cross-legged, facing her Secret Sister, Erin Janssen, on a square of cold concrete on the school playground. The February sun blanketed Scottsdale, Arizona, during the morning recess, but the cool cement still chilled Tess's legs.

"I want us to be on the team that paints the cafeteria mural this year." Erin giggled. "I've been waiting all year. Actually for two years. Do you know how much fun my brother and his friends had when they painted the mural two years ago?"

"No." Tess smiled. Erin was so excited about this.

"Well, they had a blast. And I've been looking forward to it ever since. I wouldn't miss it for anything!" She looked up toward heaven, clasped her hands, and pretended seriousness. "Oh please, oh please, Lord, let Tess and me be on the team!"

"Okay, okay, I'll try out," Tess said. "There's nothing more fun than doing things together. We have to find two more people, since four kids are on a team. And it'll definitely cause trouble with the you-know-who."

Tess nodded in the direction of the popular and powerful Coronado Club. A sick feeling unsettled her stomach. "They're going to want to do it, too."

"Maybe not," Erin said, her smile wilting just a bit. "Let's ask Katie and Joann to try out with us. Then we have to come up with a good design. One that will convince the whole sixth grade that ours is the best."

"Yeah. Katie always has good ideas."

Erin held out two pieces of colored chalk.

"What are these for?" Tess picked the green piece.

"Sketching ideas." Scraping the chalk on the concrete, Erin doodled a square.

"Uh-oh. Wait a second." Tess nodded her head toward several girls moving in their direction. "Don't draw any more."

"Just what we need, a swarm of gnats," Erin whispered. "This is like one of the ten plagues of Egypt in the Bible."

The oncoming girls were so close Tess heard them breathe.

"My goodness, it's a square, or is it two squares?" Lauren giggled in a high, unpleasant voice.

A sour mix of anger, fear, and dislike rose in Tess's throat. She looked at Lauren's perfect hairdo and then studied her four tagalongs—Colleen, Melody, Andrea, and Nancy.

They were the Coronado Club, the undisputed rulers of the sixth grade. And they knew it.

"You girls keep coloring with your baby chalk," Colleen said. "Some of us have bigger art plans, like painting the mural."

"Don't even think about trying to beat us," Lauren threatened. "You know what that would mean. War!"

Tess fixed her eyes on Colleen, who had been her best friend last summer—before Colleen backstabbed her, that is. But even she was shocked when Colleen tilted her Coke over Erin's drawing and a thin stream of soda splashed over the chalk art. "Looks like your plans are all washed up."

Only a smear of pink remained to show something used to be there. Then the Coronado Club buzzed away.

An Uneasy Team

Monday, February 3

At lunchtime Tess's stomach still churned over the trouble at recess. She opened her milk carton and took a swig, hoping it would calm her down.

"Let's get Katie and Joann," Erin said, nudging Tess off of the long, almost empty bench.

"I haven't even started to eat yet!"

"We want to invite them to try out with us, don't we?" Erin said. "So let's find them and spend our lunchtime talking about it. I think they're still in line. I'll flag them down."

How could Erin be so cheerful?

"Hey, you guys, sit with us." Erin directed Joann and Katie toward their table.

"What's up?" Joann glanced at Tess, eyebrows raised.

The others bit into their roast beef sandwiches while Erin explained. "You know how every year the sixth grade elects a team to paint the murals on the cafeteria walls?"

"Yeah, I like 'Cactus Cavalry' best." Joann chomped a baby carrot, nodding toward the east wall. Hundreds of long-armed cacti formed the border. Inside was every plant native to Arizona. "Especially the Ocotillo."

Tess loved Ocotillos, too. Their spiny, tubelike stems reminded her of cinnamon sugar churros, a long, Mexican pastry.

"What does that have to do with us?" Katie asked, eyes sparkling with anticipation.

Tess nodded. "Tell them!"

"Well—" Erin almost leaped from the table. "I want to make the team. I mean, I want us to be the team this year."

"Us?" Joann said. "As in, I am in no way artistic?"

"Gee, Joann, I thought you did everything," Tess teased. Everyone knew Joann was a super scholar-athlete. Slim and pretty, her hair was cornrowed into fine, even lines twirled into a ponytail.

"You're good," Katie reminded her best friend. "Remember how you helped paint the pots for the Christmas craft fair?"

"Well, pots are a lot different from a wall everyone stares at for four years." Joann frowned. "What do we have to do?"

"First, we make a design. Next, we have to convince our class to let us represent them. Then all the sixth graders vote on whose design they like the best. Either ours, the team from Mrs. Froget's class, or the team from Mr. Basil's class."

"And you know who that will be," Joann muttered darkly, motioning toward the Coronado Club. The girls were laughing, probably at someone else. "I don't want to get messed up with them."

"Yeah," Erin said. "We've already had a little trouble."

"Count me in," Katie said. "I'm not afraid of those goons."

"Oh, I'm so glad." Erin grinned. "You're good with art,

and everyone knows it. It'll help our chances if you're on the team."

Tess glanced at Joann's doubt-filled face. What if she refused to be on the team?

"I smell cookies. Come on, let's get some." Tess tugged Joann's slim brown arm. Before she could protest, Tess had dragged her back to the lunch line.

"Listen," she whispered urgently when she was sure Erin couldn't hear her talking. "I know you don't want to do this. Actually I didn't want to at first either. But it's really, really important to Erin."

"Why? She doesn't seem like such a competitive person." Joann sniffed, unconvinced.

"Her brother was on the team with his friends two years ago, and they have a picture of the mural hanging in their house," Tess said. "She sees it every day. Ever since then she's been dying to be on the team. It's a part of graduating sixth grade for her, you know?"

"Oh, I see. Don't we need to let Ms. M. know soon though? I mean, isn't the assembly this week?" Joann broke her peanut-butter cookie in half at the criss-cross marks and threw half away.

"Yeah. It's Friday. You know Erin can be sort of scatter-brained. She meant to ask us earlier, but she forgot."

"Oh, I don't know."

"Come on, Joann. Just because it doesn't seem important to us doesn't mean we can't do it for her," Tess pleaded, snagging a chocolate-chip cookie for herself and one for Erin.

"Oh, all right." Joann gave in. "I'll do it. I guess I could organize the campaign. I'm good at that."

"Thanks." Tess smiled at her as they strolled back to the table. Katie and Erin stacked lunch garbage on their trays.

"Let's go outside." Erin stood up, balancing a tray in each hand.

"And plan our strategy," Joann said, swallowing the last bite of her cookie.

"You mean you're in?" Turning in her excitement, Erin missed the plastic garbage pail, and her trash slid into the recycling bin instead.

"I'm in," Joann said.

"Thank you, thank you!" Erin sighed, plucking the trash out and tossing it away.

Soon the four of them were sitting on the ground, close to where Tess and Erin had sat at recess.

"Okay, who has an idea for our mural?" Joann took charge right away. Erin winked at Tess, who winked back.

"What if we have all the sixth graders dip their hands in paint and put their handprints on the wall to form the border?" Katie said. "That way everyone will have a chance to be in the mural."

"Great idea," Erin said, shifting her feet under her legs to warm them. "Depends on who I have to hold hands with on the wall." She grinned. "Do we get to choose?"

"I know who you would pick." Tess elbowed her friend. She alone knew that Erin had a crush on Scott Shearin.

"But what about the guts?" Tess said. "You know, the inside of the mural?"

"Yeah, the *guts*," Katie said, emphasizing the last word. Joann rolled her eyes. Katie knew how to gross out her friend.

"Well, what about if we put in everyone's name?" Erin offered.

"No, it's supposed to be a painting," Tess said.

"Right. What if we painted pictures of famous people

from Arizona?" Erin suggested. "Then we could say the handprints are of people who will be famous someday, too!"

"Who's famous from Arizona?" Joann asked, disbelief shadowing her voice.

"Lots of people. Steven Spielberg. Sandra Day O'Connor," Erin said.

"Who's she?" Katie asked.

"The first woman Supreme Court Justice!" Tess said. "Where have you been—Mars?"

"No," Katie said. "But drawing people is really hard. They would look dumb. How about if we draw a movie camera and put Steven Spielberg's name under it, and one of those hammer things judges use and put Sandra Day O'Connor's name under it, stuff like that?"

"It's a gavel, not a hammer," Joann said. "But that's a good idea."

"Whatever." Katie pointed to the powdery little clumps of washed-out chalk a few feet away from them. "Hey, what's that pink mess over there?"

Tess hesitated. "It's…uh, it was our drawing." Katie and Joann might as well know what they were getting into. "Until Colleen dumped her Coke on it and Lauren threatened us with a war if we tried to win the mural competition."

"I knew I shouldn't have agreed to do this," Joann moaned. Tess couldn't blame her. The Coronado Club could definitely make life hard.

three

Miss Coronado

Friday, February 7

"I'm so glad no one else from our class wanted to be on the team," Erin whispered at the end-of-the-week assembly. "It'll be hard enough to beat the Coronado Club and the team from Mrs. Froget's class."

"You made it clear to everyone how much you wanted to do it!" Tess smiled at the high pink flush of enthusiasm warming her friend's face. Then Tess scanned the gym. The basketball hoops hung down, and a vinegary smell, the scent of old sweat, filled the room. Eighty sixth graders dotted the slick wooden bleachers.

"Oh! I just remembered," Erin said. "Do you want to come over to my grandparents' house next Wednesday? They offered to pay us to finish painting their fence. My grandma said since I'm so excited about painting I can do something useful with it."

"Hmm," Tess said. "I'm taking that baby-sitting course with Melissa on Wednesday nights. I'm not sure when it starts. I'm so excited. I know I can get more baby-sitting jobs once I'm certified. I'll call her tonight; then I'll call you. Okay?"

"Okay." Erin leaned back, almost slipping between the bleachers. "I wish they would start with the team announcements. I'm hot, and I want to finish my math so I don't have so much homework this weekend."

Tess glanced at a confident Lauren flirting with someone from her class, and Tess's determination melted. How could they beat the Coronado Club? The boys were sure to vote for them.

A minute later Principal Twiddle came onstage, and the gym hushed like it did before a make-it-or-break-it free throw.

"Students," he began in his stuffy-nosed voice, "as you know, one tradition for sixth graders here at Coronado Elementary School is mural painting. Each year a team is selected to paint one of the cafeteria's walls. The mural remains for four years until another sixth-grade class paints over it. You, the student body, must choose who you want to paint the mural representing your class."

"Does it have to be a student's body? Can it be someone live?" A voice from the west bleachers caused a wave of laughter to roll up and down the gym.

"What was that? Does someone have a question?" Principal Twiddle sneezed, then took off his bifocals and scanned the crowd. "This isn't talking-out time; it's listening time."

"It was Kenny," Erin whispered to Tess.

"I know. He's such a nerd."

"Here." Bill Anderson, who was sitting behind Tess, slipped her a note. Surprised, she opened it up and began to read while the principal blew his nose.

"Just forget about the mural if you want to see seventh grade. Or we could humiliate you in front of the whole school again like we did on the bathroom mirror."

"Who's it from?" Erin whispered.

All warmth drained from Tess's heart, and icy fear rushed in instead. She tried to croak an answer, but nothing came out. She handed the note to Erin.

Erin read the note, and her face grew fierce. "Ooh, those creeps." She handed the slip of paper back.

It wasn't signed, but Tess knew the note was from the Coronado Club. Last September they had drawn a mean picture of her on the bathroom mirror for the whole school to see. Now they wanted to scare her out of the mural contest. She stuffed the note into her jeans pocket.

Principal Twiddle began to talk again.

"I have a surprise." The room hushed. Principal Twiddle's surprises weren't usually good. "We will not be voting for the mural teams today."

Erin sat straight up in alarm. Tess put her finger to her lips, shushing her friend.

"We're postponing it a few days, but for good reason. We've added a new honor. We're going to elect a Mr. and Miss Coronado to represent us at the Valley of the Sun Elementary School Banquet. All sixth graders are eligible."

Eighty mouths gaped. Mr. and Miss Coronado?

"Those who run for Mr. and Miss Coronado may not be on a team competing to paint the mural," Principal Twiddle continued. "So choose your candidates, and the remaining students may run for the mural teams.

"We'll announce the contestants Monday. Next Thursday the teachers will present their class's selection for the mural team. In two weeks we'll take final votes on both. Dismissed."

"What a shock," Erin whispered on the way back to class to vote for Mr. and Miss Coronado.

"Actually, I think it's great news!" Tess felt triumphant. Earlier dread over the note vanished like steam. "You don't think Lauren will give up the opportunity to be Miss Coronado, do you? That means she can't be on Mr. Basil's team and pressure everyone to vote for her."

Thank you, God! Tess thought.

She hugged Erin. "So unless Mrs. Froget's team comes up with something wonderful, we have it in the bag!"

"Yes!" Erin gloated and hugged her back.

four

Another Problem?

Friday Afternoon, February 7

"What happened at school today?" Molly Thomas washed a head of lettuce as Tess came up from behind and hugged her. Soon her mother's pregnant tummy wouldn't allow her to stand so close to the sink.

"Well," Tess answered, "a great thing." She didn't mention the threatening note but instead shoved it deeper into her pocket as she walked to the table.

"We get to choose Mr. and Miss Coronado this year from all the sixth graders. There's going to be a banquet or something, and whoever wins represents our school. We voted for candidates today."

"How exciting. Whom did you vote for?" Mrs. Thomas turned from the sink to face Tess, who was now doing crafts. "I'm sorry, you don't have to answer that. It's personal."

"No, it's okay. I voted for Tammy. She's a good speaker and smart. But it doesn't matter." Tess set her scissors down on a piece of heart-freckled wrapping paper. Swaddling the pretty paper around a shoebox, she slathered some glue on the sides with a thick-bristled brush.

"Why not?" Mrs. Thomas tore the lettuce and put it into a salad bowl.

"Because Lauren will win anyway. She always does. She's the worst possible person to represent the school, but everyone will fall to their knees and vote her in anyway. But," Tess said with a smile, "that means it will be easier for us to win the murals."

"Pearls! I say, who's winning pearls?" Eight-year-old Tyler, Tess's little brother, slid into the room in his stocking feet.

"Murals, not pearls," Tess enunciated, throwing a cherry-red pompom at him.

"Blimey, a bit touchy today, eh?" Tyler often spoke in a thick, imitation British accent, preparing for his future career in Scotland Yard. He glanced at the table where she worked. "What are you doin', mate?"

"Making valentines."

"Ooh, Tess and her honey, sitting in a tree, K-I-S-S-I-N-G," Tyler sang out. Tess looked at her mother, who suppressed a smile.

"This is for Erin, you dustball. Maybe you make valentines for your honey." Tess's face was brighter red than the wrapping paper. She hadn't told anyone, but she was thinking of sending Tom, Erin's fourteen-year-old brother, a secret valentine.

"Yuck. Girls? Useless. Except for cleaning."

"If you think that, I have a job for you." Mrs. Thomas handed Tyler a broom. "Sweep up please."

"Can't Tess? I need to trap some crickets." Hercules, Tyler's pet horned toad, gulped a cricket or two each day.

"No, that's your new job," Mrs. Thomas said. "I'd better scribble in that business meeting for next Wednesday," she mumbled to herself, walking to the wall calendar.

"Oh yeah, I almost forgot," Tess said. "If my baby-sitting class doesn't start next week, can I go to Erin's grandparents' house after school Wednesday? They're going to pay us to help paint their fence."

"Don't you know when that class starts yet? We've talked about this three or four times already. You have to stay on top of these things. Call Melissa right now and find out. And see if you can carpool. I'm not running a taxi service." Her mother wiped her brow. "I'm going to watch the news till Dad gets home." She pushed up her sleeves and filled a glass from the water cooler before heading into the family room.

Mom sure was moody. Tess reached into her pocket and fished out the crumpled-up note from the Coronado Club. Fear chilled her.

On her way to her room she stopped off in the bathroom, thought for a minute, then tossed the note. She aimed for the garbage, but it was a dead ringer into the toilet. She flushed and saluted as it swirled down the pipes. So long.

Then she walked to her room so she could call in private. As she flipped the switch that turned on both her light and radio, she kicked her shoes into the closet.

Untacking a scrap of paper from her bulletin board that contained Melissa's number, she dialed the phone. Melissa had invited Tess to work with her in the church nursery a few months ago. Since Tess's parents weren't Christians, Tess went to church with Erin and her family. It was nice to have Melissa as a friend there, too.

"Hello?"

"Um, is Melissa there?"

"This is Melissa."

"This is Tess. Sorry, I never know if it's you or your sister."

"It's okay." Melissa still didn't sound like herself.

"I was calling to check on the baby-sitting class. Am I signed up? Does it start next Wednesday? Do you want to carpool?" Tess shot all her questions at Melissa without pausing.

Then a long silence stretched like a piece of well-chewed gum. "Uh, I asked Terri, you know, my best friend? Her mom is in charge," Melissa finally said. "Four people are already signed up for the class. That's supposed to be the limit." Melissa's words rushed out so fast Tess could barely understand.

"But I asked Terri to include you. They've had five before. So I don't think it will be a problem, but she didn't get back to me. I'll call her; then I'll let you know."

Tess couldn't figure out Melissa's voice. Usually she was calm, but tonight she sounded nervous and hurried.

"Okay. Well, let me know if it's a problem," Tess said.

"All right. I have to go eat now. Call you later. Bye." Melissa hung up without waiting for Tess to answer. Confused and hurt, Tess slipped the phone back into the cradle.

five

Surprise, Surprise

Monday, February 10

Near the end of the day Monday Erin lifted the top of her desk to stuff her health book and some loose papers into her backpack. "I guess I'd better pack up. My mom will be here in a few minutes." She moaned. "I don't know why my appointment had to be today. I'll miss the announcement!"

"You're coming over after dinner. I can tell you then," Tess said. "Besides, will it be any big surprise? Lauren will be one of the nominees, and she'll win."

"I suppose you're right. I just don't want to go to the dentist. What if he drills and it hurts? Plus I hate that fluoride goop. It gags me." Sticking her tongue out in disgust before zipping up her pack, Erin said, "I'll see you at six-thirty, okay?"

Tess nodded, and Erin handed a pass to Ms. Martinez and left.

Tess scribbled a cartoon on the back of her social studies book cover. Maybe she could draw a cartoon for Tom for a secret valentine. But then, if he saw her drawing anywhere else, he might guess it had come from her. Then she would roll over and die. She had better give this valentine some more thought.

Five minutes before class was to end, Ms. M. allowed the students to pack their backpacks for home.

"Take your seats and settle down please," Ms. M. called out. Her glossy black hair was twisted up into a pretzel and secured by silver hair rods. Tess thought they looked like chopsticks, but she would never tell Ms. M. She was the best teacher in the sixth grade.

"It's time for announcements. When Principal Twiddle finishes speaking, please remain in your seats until the final bell."

Tess plopped her backpack on top of her closed desk and laid her head down on it. Maybe she would rest after school. Oh yeah, it was piano lesson day. They would have to take Tyler for his lesson.

The speaker system crackled to life. "Hello? Can you hear me?" the principal shouted into the speaker.

"Yeah, they can hear you in California!" Russell shouted, his hands covering his ears. He flopped on the floor like a landed fish. Tess lifted her head and watched his clowning. So embarrassing. Didn't he have any pride?

"In your seat please," Ms. M. told him, and reluctantly he slid back into his chair.

Principal Twiddle continued, "I'd like to announce the nominees for Mr. and Miss Coronado. Ladies first. For Miss Coronado you've nominated Jillian Benson, Lauren Mayfield, Melody Shirowsky, and Tess Thomas."

Tess shot up in her chair, stunned, and looked around the room. Me? There must be some mistake!

Her classmates grinned at her or gave her the thumbs up, calling, "Way to go, Tess."

Her mouth completely dried up, and she flushed with fear, excitement, and confusion. How could this be? With shaky hands she grasped her pack. She could barely see straight. She missed the nominees for Mr. Coronado.

The other students left, but Tess hung back for a minute to talk with Ms. Martinez. Ms. M's silky peach blouse highlighted her creamy tan skin. When she walked, a slight scent of fruit perfumed the air. Somehow that calmed Tess right now.

"Congratulations, Miss Thomas."

"Uh, thanks. Can I ask you something?" Tess shifted her backpack and looked Ms. M. in the eye.

"Anything."

"Do you think there was a mistake? I mean, that they counted the votes wrong?"

"No, there's no mistake. Why?"

"It's just that, you know, I'm not really popular, and I don't know why I would be voted in with those others."

"Well, our class likes you. They certainly got to know you better at your party last month. I even heard Kenny and Russell say how much fun they had. The other votes may have been split between many girls."

"I guess so." Tess zipped up her sweat jacket and started for the door.

"It's an honor, and I'd like to see you represent Coronado. Good luck!" Ms. M. waved before turning back to her papers.

❄

"Fancy that, you're nominated," Tyler said as he climbed into the car. "Good luck."

"I don't know. It seems unreal," Tess mumbled.

"Say, old bean, I'm kidding. You deserve it as much as anyone."

"I'm confused," Mrs. Thomas said, jerking the car into gear. "Tyler, your accent isn't helping things. What are you two talking about?" The Jeep bounced over the edge of the curb.

"Mom, slow down! I don't want to run anyone over!" Tess shouted. Of course it was her day to sit in the front, where everyone could see her as her mother tore away!

"We have to get Tyler to piano lessons in five minutes," her mom said. "Now, what's this nomination about?" Mrs. Thomas turned to face Tess. Her mom's emerald green eyes were bright with curiosity. Being pregnant only made her mother prettier, Tess thought.

"Remember I told you about Mr. and Miss Coronado? They made the announcement today, and I'm one of the nominees. Can you believe it?"

"Tess, what a wonderful privilege!" Her mother leaned over and kissed Tess's hair. "Of course you deserve to win! When's the final vote?"

The shock dimmed, and a warm glow began to spread over Tess's skin. Why shouldn't she be nominated, after all? It would only be fair that a regular person win. "Next week," she said.

"Who else was nominated?"

"Jillian Benson, Melody Shirowsky, and Lauren. You know what's funny? All the popular people will have to split their votes between Melody and Lauren, so maybe Jillian and I have a chance."

"Wonderful." Mrs. Thomas pulled up in front of the music academy. "We'll be back in an hour to pick you up," she said as Tyler jumped out. "Here's the check for this month. Please give it to Mr. Paul."

"Okay," Tyler grabbed the check and a handful of music books from his mother.

"Let's get a soda while we wait." Mrs. Thomas drove to Wendy's and parked the car, gently this time, much to Tess's relief. They ordered two drinks and some fries to share, then grabbed a booth by a window.

"I'll bet Erin is tickled about your nomination," her mother said.

"She doesn't know yet. She had to go to the dentist and left school a few minutes early." Tess beamed. Of course her friend would be glad for her!

"Well, I'm sure she'll be overjoyed. She's coming to do homework tonight, right? You can tell her then. We'll celebrate together."

Her mother dipped a fry into the paper ketchup cup. "Of course, she'll have to find someone else for the mural team."

Oh no! Tess suddenly remembered. "Mom, I can't run for Miss Coronado!" She nearly knocked over her soda. "If I do, Erin will have to drop out."

"Oh honey, it's not that serious, is it? Can't they find someone to replace you?"

The picture of Erin praying at recess for them to be together on the team popped into Tess's head, an unwelcome intrusion. "I—I don't know. Maybe." Even as she said it, doubt clouded her spirit. She popped a hot fry into her mouth, savoring the little beads of salt as they melted on her tongue.

When they had asked if they could represent the class, no one had argued or even seemed to want to do it. It had seemed like a blessing then, but was it now?

"You'll have to think carefully before dropping out. People voted for you because they want you to represent them, and you might let them down."

"I know," Tess groaned. "But whether I drop out or not, Lauren will probably win. She's so snobby she's the last person that should represent our school. Not that I'm great or anything.

"Plus, Erin is looking forward to doing this together. You know, we do stuff without each other, like her riding and my baby-sitting class. And with our families. We like to do some special things together. She practically begged me to do this with her. It's the most important part of sixth grade for her. I can't let her down."

"I understand." Her mother placed her hand over Tess's. "You have a lot to think about. Let's get some gas and wait for Tyler." She patted her tummy. "I shouldn't have eaten that. We'll need to have dinner early so we'll be finished when Erin arrives."

The thought echoed in Tess's mind. *When Erin arrives.* Tess checked her watch, and her hopes crashed. She had less than three hours to figure out what she was going to do.

six

Love Is...

Monday Night, February 10

"Come on in." Tess bulldozed a pile of dirty clothes, some old papers, and her jacket out of the way so the door would open wide enough to let Erin into Tess's bedroom.

"Wooee, you have a lot of stuff in here." Erin giggled, tossing her jacket onto Tess's bed.

"I know. I'm supposed to clean it up before bedtime. But I made room for us to lie on the floor and do homework and make our valentines. Did you bring your stuff?"

"Yes." Erin unzipped her backpack and pulled out a handful of valentine cards. "Should we do these first or the homework?"

"Um, the homework. Let's get it out of the way." Tess chewed on her pencil stub, knowing what else she should get out of the way. The wood tasted bitter, like the choice before her. She just didn't have the courage to tell Erin.

"Did you finish the health homework?" Erin asked.

"Yes. I'm so glad they didn't do the 'Your Wonderful Body' chapter. I can imagine what Kenny and Russell would have to say about that. How embarrassing."

"I heard they save that for the end of the year. Then they split up the boys and girls, and you see a movie." Erin pulled out her book from her backpack and smoothed a slightly wrinkled paper before writing on it.

"Well, the movie sounds dorky, too."

Erin scribbled an answer. "That reminds me. Are you planning to make a valentine for my brother?"

"What? 'Dorky' reminded you?" Tess giggled. "I don't know. I mean, I wouldn't want him to know. What if he found out?"

"I won't tell him. You can trust me with anything! We're Secret Sisters, right?" Erin smiled at Tess. "Here, I brought you something." She handed Tess a tiny package.

"What is it?" Tess eagerly unwrapped the lacy box.

"An early valentine's present. When I saw this, I knew I had to have one, and so did you." Erin looked on eagerly as Tess lifted the lid.

From a soft pillow of cotton she lifted out a silver charm. Oh no, a paintbrush! Her heart cracked.

"Oh, Erin, I don't know what to say." *Especially since I might not paint.*

"Put it on! It's to remind us of painting the mural. I know we haven't won yet, but I'm sure we will because I've been praying. It's not every day you see a paintbrush charm, you know!" Erin held up her arm and shook her wrist. Her charms jingled and glittered. "Mine's already on."

What could she do? Tess took out the charm and caressed it, unwilling to attach it to the charm bracelet she always wore. The two of them never took off their identical bracelets—except to swap them with each other, of course.

A thin sheen of sweat covered Tess's forehead. She

swallowed the lump in her throat, but it came back. "I need to tell you something."

"Sure, anything. You're okay, aren't you?"

"Yeah, I'm okay. It's just that, well, you know today they announced the nominees for Miss Coronado?"

"I completely forgot to ask you who was nominated. Lauren, right? And who else?" Erin leaned forward to get the scoop.

"Melody Shirowsky and Jillian Anderson." Tess didn't look into her friend's face.

"Jillian! Good. I like her." Erin leapt to her feet. "And since both Melody and Lauren are running, we're almost sure to win the murals! Thank you, Lord!" She giggled. "I never thought I'd thank the Lord for allowing Lauren to win something."

She looked at Tess's lukewarm face. "What's the matter? Aren't you excited?"

"Well, there's something else you should know." Tess breathed out the words. "I was the fourth nominee."

"What did you say?"

"Me. I was the fourth nominee." Tess set the charm back into the box and looked up.

"I can't believe it." Erin sank into the carpet, a blank look whitewashing her face. "I mean, it's not that I don't think you deserve it."

"I know what you mean. I can't believe it myself. But it really is an honor, you know."

"Yes," Erin said, "Well, I'm happy for you. Really, I am." A silent minute ticked by before she continued, "I guess this means you'll drop out of the mural team competition." Tess saw Erin struggle not to cry, but her face was downcast, and her eyelashes glistened.

"I'm not sure." Tess scooted next to her. "I mean, I'd like to do the mural team. I know you really want to do it, too. But who wants Lauren to be Miss Coronado? And, well, I guess I think it might be kind of fun. I'll bet you guys could find someone else to do the mural with you. A better artist than me even."

Erin slipped her health book into her backpack and looked up. "I would be sad to do the mural without you. If we even won. But I think you should do what you want to. Maybe Michelle will try out with us."

"Yeah, she's a good artist. But," Tess drew out her words, "I'm not sure what I'm going to do."

"What do you mean?" A light flickered in Erin's eyes.

"Run for Miss Coronado or not. I thought I'd already know, but I don't."

Erin placed her hand over Tess's. "It's all right. I'll be okay, and so will the others. There isn't anyone I'd rather have represent our school than you." She plucked the paint charm back up and quietly handed it to Tess. "You can still put this on, since you're coming to paint the fence with me Wednesday, right?"

"Right," Tess said. "It was so weird," she rushed on, seeing a chance to change the subject. "Yesterday at church I asked Melissa if the baby-sitting class started this Wednesday, to find out if I could paint the fence with you. And she said, 'Next Wednesday.' But before I could ask her to carpool or whatever, she ran over to Terri and turned her back to me."

"That doesn't sound like Melissa," Erin stammered, still not herself. "But I'm glad you can come. You can bring your valentine for my brother. I'll sneak it to him sometime when he won't know I was the delivery person."

In spite of the small talk, tension fogged the air.

"Okay, then let's start making them. Did you bring one for Scott?" Tess teased.

"Yes, but I bought one for everyone in the class," Erin defended.

"I bet you picked his out first," Tess said. She shook her finger to say, "Naughty, naughty."

"Actually," Erin said, "I picked yours out first." She bent down to sort through her cards. Tess's jumbled feelings overwhelmed her.

Later that night after Erin had gone home, Tess reached under her bed to pull out the valentine box she was making for Erin. It had started out as a simple cardboard box. Now she had lacquered the sides with beautiful paper on the themes of love and friendship, leaving a wide open spot on the lid for a Bible verse she had heard and wanted to look up.

Pulling her red calligraphy pen out of her junk drawer, she thumbed through the concordance in the back of her Bible looking for the verse. Love. Hmm. Holy cow! There must be two hundred verses. Okay, maybe not that many, but a lot. After reading several dozen, she found the one she wanted.

Uncapping her pen she started to copy 1 Corinthians 13 onto the cloudy white paper on the box top. As she slowly inked each word, a different verse she had just read ran through her mind: Romans 12:10. "Love each other like brothers and sisters. Give your brothers and sisters more honor than you want for yourselves."

She finished the box and slid it under her bed before kissing her parents good-night. Afterward, on an impulse, she stopped in the hallway at the game closet to drag out the dress-up box.

"I haven't looked in here in a long time," she muttered to herself, tossing out a pirate's hat and a long pink feather boa. "Who knows if it's even here?"

Finally, she found what she was looking for, a glittering, jeweled tiara she had worn as a dress-up princess. She hurriedly stuffed the other things back into the box and the box into the closet. Then she ran to her room with the tiara under her arm.

Once there, she set it carefully on her head and looked into the mirror. "Ladies and gentlemen, I present to you our first Miss Coronado, Tess Thomas!" She practiced a movie-star smile, curtsying. The tiara looked good.

seven

Growing Up

Tuesday, February 11

Tess's baby-sitting job the next day wasn't as easy as she had hoped.

A red checker sailed over her head, striking the Kim family's cat. "Hey, you guys, who's throwing checkers?" She ran into the family room to stare at Jerry and Joe.

"Not me." Jerry, the oldest, stood up. "It was him." He pointed at his younger brother.

"Well, you just hit the cat," Tess said. "How can I make your snack if you can't play nicely together for five minutes?"

"You're taking too long," Joe whined. "I want to play."

"The popcorn won't pop any faster. You'll just have to be patient." Both boys nodded their agreement, and Tess returned to the kitchen.

"I wonder if they talk about cat abuse in that baby-sitting course," she mumbled, pouring apple cider into three glasses. A minute or two later the microwave beeped, and she grabbed the bag, ripping open the top. Steam rushed out, and she was careful not to burn her hand as she dumped it into a bowl. After shaking on a thin coat of parmesan cheese, she walked back into the family room.

"Here." She sat down on the floor. "What do you want to play?"

"I want to play Trouble," Joe said.

"I don't. I want to play Nintendo. Come on." Jerry dragged the Super Nintendo set across the family room floor to where they sat. "Look, I have a lot of CDs."

"I don't care about your CDs!" Joe tossed a checker at his brother this time, conking him on the head. "I want to play Trouble." Jerry reached toward Joe, but Tess caught his arm in time.

"Whoa there." She checked her watch. "Your mom is going to be home in fifteen minutes, so we don't have time to do both."

"Well, I'm the oldest, so I get to pick," Jerry said. "And I pick Nintendo."

"Being the oldest doesn't mean you always get to pick," Tess said. "I should know, I'm the oldest, too."

"Yippee. That means Trouble?" Joe jumped up and down.

"What do you say?" Tess looked at Jerry. "Can we do what your brother wants? Remember," she said, "I'm coming back next week, and we can play Nintendo first."

"Oh, all right." Jerry shoved the control box away. "I guess so." Fifteen minutes later Mrs. Kim came home and found the three of them playing Trouble.

"You three look like you're having a good time," she said, setting an overstuffed shopping bag on the floor.

"We are!" Jerry said. Even Jerry had a good time popping the center down on the Trouble game and moving his guys around the clear plastic board.

"Did everything go okay?"

"Yes," Tess answered. "They did great."

"Oh good." Mrs. Kim handed some folded-up bills to Tess who stuffed them into her front jeans pocket. "So you'll be back next Tuesday?"

"Yes." Tess pulled her sweat jacket on. "Same time?"

"Same time," Mrs. Kim said as she opened the front door. "Do you need a ride home?"

"No, my mom said I could walk before dark. 'Bye, guys," Tess called into the family room.

"'Bye, Tess," Joe answered.

"And don't forget we play Nintendo first next time," Jerry added. Tess smiled. He hadn't forgotten.

She walked down the street, dusky light casting mailbox shadows on the pavement. Unfolding the bills, she counted her earnings. Great! After giving 10 percent to her church, she could stick most of this into her savings account. Slowly but surely she was saving enough for the Lazy Bar K. She and Erin were planning to go to camp at the famous dude ranch. In fact, they already had their deposits in. Riding together was one of the things they liked to do best.

"I hope we can ride tomorrow," she said to no one in particular. She hurried a bit now, as the oncoming night ate up the remaining daylight. Painting the fence would be fun, too. And more money! After walking by three more houses, she opened the door to her home.

"I'm here," she called.

"We're in the family room," her mother answered.

"I'll be right there." Tess hung up her jacket and went into her room to put her money in her top desk drawer. She kicked off her shoes and socks and grabbed a bottle of nail polish before joining her family.

"How was it?" Tess's dad asked as she sat on the floor. Mr. Thomas was a tall, athletic man. Tess looked like him. They had the same shade of hair.

"Fine. The boys did okay." Tess rolled some lint from between her toes, left over from the socks.

"You want this?" she joked to her brother, pointing at the little pile.

"Why on earth would he want that?" her mother said.

"Big Al and I are having a toe cheese contest." Tyler shook his head. "But it has to be from our own feet. So, sorry to say, can't accept your offer."

"What are you talking about?" Mr. Thomas turned his eyes from the game on TV and faced Tyler.

"Big Al and I are saving our toe cheese for a whole year to see who collects the most."

"Where are you keeping these specimens?" his dad asked.

"In a Tupperware bowl. In my desk drawer."

"Just don't put it back in the kitchen when you're through," his dad chuckled.

Tess shook the bottle of polish and unscrewed the top.

"Put a piece of newspaper underneath your feet before you paint your toenails," her father admonished. "I don't want polish all over the carpet."

Tess rolled her eyes but grabbed a section of the newspaper from the stack next to her mother. She brushed some Turquoise Moonlight on her big toe.

"I say, your toes are odd," Tyler said. "They're not straight like the rest of the family's. They're—crooked!"

"Oh, leave me alone," Tess grumped. It was true. She hoped the polish wouldn't make that more noticeable.

"I can't believe how much those guys fight," she said.

"Who?" her father asked.

"Jerry and Joe. They fight about everything."

"You should listen to you and your brother sometime." Her mother closed her newspaper and looked at Tess. "And you were worse when you were younger."

"I say, we've matured," Tyler said.

"They fight about who gets to go first, who gets to pick the snack, who gets to choose what we'll do."

"It's part of growing up," her dad said, "doing what others want to and not always what you want. They'll grow out of it." Tess listened carefully, her mind flying back to the verse she had read last night about honoring your sister more than yourself.

She capped the polish. "Mom, Dad, I think I need to talk to you about something."

eight

Decisions

Wednesday, February 12

The next day after school, Tess waved at Erin to go on. "I'll meet you outside. I want to talk with Ms. M. for a minute."

"Okay." Erin strode out the door.

"Yes, Tess?" Ms. M. took off her glasses. Tess liked her better without them.

"I have something to tell you. It's about the Miss Coronado race."

"Wonderful. Do you want help preparing a speech?" Ms. M. beamed. "I'm so pleased someone from my class was nominated."

"Well, that's just it." Ms. M. wouldn't be so pleased when she heard what Tess had to say. "I'm dropping out."

"What? Tess, I'm surprised. Why would you do that?" Ms. M.'s eyes never left Tess's.

"Well, I really want to do it. Believe me! I'd love to win, and I'm thankful everyone voted me in. It makes me feel so liked. Which I never felt before." Tess blushed.

"But…"

"But Erin wants me to do the mural with her. And I

can't try out for both. So I'm dropping Miss Coronado." It sounded so simple. It didn't feel that way.

"I understand how much you like Erin, Tess. And I think it's admirable that you would do that. But you can't always sacrifice what you want for something someone else wants."

"I know. I don't always. This time, though, it's really important to Erin that we do the mural together. At least try to do it, even if we don't win. She's never asked me for anything else."

"I understand, and although I'm disappointed, I respect your decision. I'll let Principal Twiddle know." Ms. M. stood up and held out her hand for a shake.

"Thanks!" Tess shook her hand. Wow, she had never shaken anyone's hand before! She smiled for the first time that day. This morning, she hadn't really been sure she wanted to go through with her decision, but as the day had worn on, she grew more sure this was right. Now she knew it was.

"Good-bye, Ms. M."

"Good-bye, Miss Thomas. I'll see you tomorrow." Tess slung her pack over her shoulder and walked outside to tell Erin the news that would make her day.

nine

High Note and Baby Grand

Wednesday, February 12

Tess held off telling her the news until she and Erin were alone. So she said nothing for the thirty-five-minute drive to Erin's grandparents' ranch.

As soon as they arrived, Erin jumped out of the Suburban. "Let's look at the horses first thing."

Tess followed Erin to the six-stall barn, where a dry, slightly green scent of fresh hay curled around her nose. She felt like sneezing. The hay crunched under her feet, alerting the horses. They stamped a bit, standing nose-out toward the middle of the barn. "What did you name the new horses?"

"Well, the mare is called High Note because she's a good jumper. We got to name the foal. She's called Baby Grand."

"Oh, how sweet." Tess slowly walked toward the foal so as not to scare her. After letting the little one get used to her for a minute, she petted the damp, velvet nose and the smooth, downy coat between the foal's ears.

"It's okay, honey," she said before turning to Erin. "Can we give her a treat?"

"Apple pieces." Erin reached into a tin pail next to Baby Grand's stall. "Here." She placed several moon-shaped apple slices in Tess's open hand. Tess held her hand under the foal's mouth, and soon Baby Grand nuzzled her palm and nibbled the apple pieces.

"What kind of horses are they? I mean, what breed?"

"They're paints."

Tess looked over at High Note, her glossy black coat splashed with creamy white. "Hey, they do look painted. That is too funny. Do you think we could ride later?"

"Sure, after we finish the fence. Tom and Josh did the first half, so it won't take too long. You can ride Dustbuster, and I'll ride High Note. Nobody rides Baby Grand yet."

"Let's hurry up then!"

"Okay. I need to ask my grandpa where the brushes are." They walked toward the ranch-style home, which was slung low over sprawling acreage. When Tess daydreamed, she imagined she lived in a house like this with a stable of horses outside and a dusky Western interior. A brittle tumbleweed cartwheeled into her path, and she kicked it, almost tripping over a stray prickly pear cactus as she did.

Five minutes later Erin's grandpa set up the paint and handed them two brushes, and they started to work.

Tess drew the paintbrush across the wooden beams, back and forth, imagining she was grooming Dustbuster or maybe High Note. Erin seemed to be deep in thought, but Tess couldn't hold in her surprise any longer.

"I have great news."

"What?" Erin stopped painting.

"I dropped out of the Miss Coronado race. So we can

compete to do the mural together." Tess jingled her charm bracelet. "You know, sisters doing everything together."

Erin balanced her brush across the top of the paint can, ran to Tess, and hugged her. "Thanks, Tess. You didn't have to do that. You're the best friend in the whole world."

"Well yeah, I'm your best friend anyway," Tess flushed with pleasure. It felt good to do something for someone else.

"What made you change your mind?" Erin asked. "Just out of curiosity."

"It's sort of weird. When I was baby-sitting yesterday, those boys fought about everything: who would pick the snack, who would pick the game, whatever. So when I got home, I told my dad about it. He said when they grow up they'll let others go first."

"Then—and this is so weird—I couldn't stop thinking about a Bible verse. Does that ever happen to you?" Tess dipped her brush into the milky white paint and sloshed some on the top rail.

"Sometimes. It can be sort of annoying. Like I need to do what the verse says, or I can't concentrate on anything else." Erin drew her brush across a post just a few feet from Tess.

"Exactly! It was about letting your brother or sister get honor, not yourself." Tess didn't look up but kept painting absentmindedly with an almost dry brush. "I don't want to sound like Holy Hero or anything, but I felt God telling me to do the murals with you. We really better win now, or I will have given that up for nothing!"

Erin's face fell. "Will you hate me if we don't? Will you be sorry you did this for me?"

"Of course I won't hate you! You're my sister. But I want it to be worthwhile, you know?"

"Yeah, well, I'll pay you back by delivering your valentine to my brother," Erin teased. She picked up her brush again and finished one post before following the fence line to the next.

"I don't know. What if he found out it was from me? I'd feel stupid coming over to your house." High Note whinnied, and Tess painted faster. She wanted to ride.

"How would he find out? I could sneak it into the mailbox in the morning. He wouldn't know who sent it."

"I guess. I want to do it, but..."

"Come on, Tess. Don't be a chicken. I'm sending one to Scott."

"He's in class."

"I think you should do it," Erin insisted, grinning at her friend.

"Okay. It's in my backpack." Tess moved over to the next rail. They were almost done.

"See! You're busted. You were planning all along to give it to him," Erin gloated.

"Listen here, if you want any help with this mural thing, you had better stop hassling me right now!" Tess teased her friend.

"We're going to win now, I just know it." Erin took Tess's hands and danced around. "Lauren's out of the way, and we're going to win. We can hang our posters up Friday at lunch so everyone can see our design before Monday's vote."

"Who's making the posters? Are we supposed to do that?"

"Joann's doing it. Her dad has a color copier at his work,

so he said we could use it. Katie sketched out the idea, and Joann will bring them on Friday."

Erin continued, "If the Coronado Club wants war, they can have it. They'll never win, especially without Lauren!" Erin drew her paintbrush into the air like a samurai sword.

"On guard." Tess raised high her brush, dripping with white paint. She and Erin sparred for a minute, paint flying all over both of them and landing in splotches on the ground like puddles of melted vanilla ice cream.

Erin broke out in giggles as she looked at Tess. "You look like one of the horses—covered with paint!"

Tess whipped her brush into the air, keeping hold of the handle but letting the paint splatter all over Erin. "Now we're Secret *Painted* Sisters."

Erin looked down at herself and then at her friend and laughed even harder.

"I hope this washes out!" They both said at the same time. Then they started to laugh all over again.

ten

Poster Power

Friday, February 14

"Tess, are you signed up for the baby-sitting seminar or not? I have to make plans, you know." Mrs. Thomas shook a spoonful of sugar over a bowl of corn flakes.

"I don't know for sure. It's probably okay or Melissa would have told me. I'll get the details at church on Sunday or for sure at the party Sunday night."

"Drat!" Tyler whined, dropping a vitamin-dusted cricket into Hercules' cage. "You get to go to another party?" Hercules lunged at the dazed insect. As the lizard snapped his powerful jaws, he halved the victim in one bite.

"That's so gross." Tess turned away. "Do you have to bring him in the kitchen?"

"Where else would he eat breakfast?" Tyler said. "But you didn't answer me. Are you going to another party?"

"Yep. It's a Golden Rule party for the sixth, seventh, and eighth graders. Sunday night at church." Tess shoveled in another bite of corn flakes.

"I wish I could go." Tyler pushed his chair back and stood up.

"Sorry. I think my church has other stuff for your age. Do you want me to ask Erin's brother Josh?"

"Okay," Tyler said. "I'll be ready to go to school in a second." He went to put Hercules in his room. Tess didn't look at her mother, and her mother didn't say anything to her. It was the first time she had ever mentioned—or had even thought about—inviting Tyler to church.

"Well, today's the day we put up the posters!" she said. "The ones to convince the sixth grade to vote for us. I hope ours look good. Katie drew them, and Joann's dad made color copies at work."

"I'll be thinking of you, honey." Her mother kissed Tess's cheek, bumping her round tummy into Tess.

"Hi, baby." Tess patted her mother's tummy. "Hey, the baby kicked me! I felt it."

"So it did." Her mother smiled. "That little one kicked all night. No wonder I'm tired!"

Tess left her hand there for a minute to feel a few more kicks. "'Bye, baby!" she called toward her mom's stomach.

"Have a good day." Her mother shooed her toward the door where Tess met Tyler for the short walk to school.

It was too cold to go outside for morning recess. So Tess and her friends stayed in and talked.

"This is the worst part of February." Joann shuffled a small stack of cards away from her. "It's such a mushball day anyway, I mean, Valentines. Really. As if we can't tell people we like them at other times of the year?"

"Have anyone special in mind?" Katie teased.

"No, I have too many plans for my life to worry about boys," Joann answered. Then she softened. "But thank you for your valentine. It was the nicest one I've ever received." She smiled at her friend. "Let's go get a book." They walked over to the bookshelf, leaving Tess and Erin alone.

"How about you?" Tess whispered to Erin. "Any special valentines?"

"Yes," Erin sneaked one out of the beautiful box Tess had presented to her that morning. "What do you think?" She handed Tess a pink card with a red heart figure riding a dirt bike. "You really rev up my day!" it said. Then in carefully written letters: "From Scott."

"Do you think it means anything?" Erin asked.

Tess wasn't sure, but she didn't want to discourage her friend either. "Maybe. I mean, he obviously thinks you're fun to be around." She smiled at Erin's relief. "Hey, that reminds me. Did you put my valentine to your brother in the mailbox?"

"Yes. But I probably won't know his reaction until after school. My mom won't check the mailbox until later."

"Promise me you'll call me the minute you hear anything, okay?" Tess clutched her friend's hand.

"Of course!" Erin squeezed her hand in return.

It seemed as if lunchtime would never arrive; the day dragged its feet as the girls counted the hours on the wide-faced classroom clock. Finally the lunch bell rang, and the girls raced out of the room—not to eat lunch but to hang their posters.

"I just know they'll love our idea." Erin taped one every three or four feet. "Katie, you did such a great job on these. Especially the handprints. That way everyone gets to be a part of the mural!"

A few minutes later they noticed the Coronado Club streaming into the hallway.

"Look," Tess whispered, "they have a whole boatload of posters, and they blew them up really big!"

Colleen taped some over the drinking fountain, and Lauren placed one nearly on top of one Erin had just hung.

"My goodness, who are the 'Double Double S's'?" she sneered, referring to the name of the girls' team. She didn't overlap their poster, but the size of hers and how close it was placed dwarfed the ones Katie had sketched.

"It's us," Tess answered. Of course she wasn't going to tell them it stood for Double Secret Sisters. "How nice of you to help Colleen, Andrea, and Nancy hang posters. But are you supposed to be helping at all? I mean, I think it's against the rules."

"Why would it be against the rules?" Lauren plastered another poster right next to theirs, overlapping a little this time.

"You can move that over; we were here first," Erin said.

"Sorry, *honey*," Lauren said disrespectfully. She moved it over, and Tess got a good look at their poster.

It was pretty. Most of the border was squiggles of silver, gold, and bronze. Probably because so much mining was done in Arizona. And the inside showed a big circle of students holding hands around a campfire. She read aloud some neatly printed words. "'If we win, we'll buy pizza for the whole sixth grade on the day we paint the mural.' Are you guys kidding?"

"No, of course not. My daddy offered to pay for it as a celebration," Lauren said.

"But why would your daddy pay? You're not even on the team," Katie said.

"Of course she is." Colleen came up next to Lauren.

She stood so close to she that she could have counted the freckles on Colleen's face if she had wanted to.

"I thought you were running for Miss Coronado." Tess faced Lauren.

"Well, I know everyone wanted me to. But it only lasts for a year, and the mural lasts for four. So I'd be more famous. Besides, I don't want to miss the chance to paint with my very best bud." She linked arms with Colleen.

Lauren added, "Melody can win Miss Coronado, and we'll win the mural. It's only right that the Coronado Club take it all."

She dragged Colleen, who was giggling, down the hall to hang more posters. Tess stared at Erin, whose mouth hung open in disbelief with no sound coming out. The tape dispenser slipped from Katie's fingers and clattered to the floor.

eleven

Confusion

Saturday, February 15

Tess's dad sat on the concrete steps leading from the house into the garage, lacing up his hiking boots. Running his fingers through his thinning hair before putting on a Phoenix Suns cap, he turned and looked at Tess. "Ready to go, Cupcake?"

"Dad, I asked you not to call me that! I'm twelve now, you know." Tess yanked on her own boots, pulling the red laces as tight as possible so she wouldn't repeat last month's accident when she had twisted her ankle hiking Squaw Peak.

"Where are we hiking?" she asked. It was superstitious, she knew, but she hadn't wanted to go back to Squaw Peak since her accident. What if she fell again? It had been a painful fall.

"I think we'll do Camelback, if you're up for it." Dad opened the garage door and climbed into the car. Tess got in, too, and fastened her seat belt.

"Fine with me." Their weekly hikes had started out as just a fun time together, but now they had another reason to go. They had signed up to hike the Rim-to-Rim across the Grand Canyon this coming May.

Tess rubbed her hand over her leg, flexing her muscles. The calves were tighter, stronger. She would be ready.

It didn't take long to drive to Camelback Mountain. Dark purple dawn warmed to pink as the sun rose over the mountains to the east. The early morning frost evaporated on the car window as she watched the scenery unfold. Bushy Palo Verdes crowded the area between sidewalk and street, their blue-barked stems stripped and skeletal. Tiny hummingbirds swirled through the air, a whirlwind of needle beaks and knobby bodies.

"Why do you think Grandma Kate likes hummingbirds so much?" Tess asked her dad. Tess's grandma strung glass globes of red sugar water from her patio so the hummingbirds could drink.

"Hmm. Maybe because they're small and cute. Or maybe because they're always moving, like Grandma," her dad answered.

"Like she used to," Tess said. Age had slowed Grandma down.

"Like she used to," her dad agreed. They pulled into the parking lot, locked the car, and began to walk up the gently sloping trail.

It was ten or fifteen minutes before either of them spoke.

"Did you get your posters up yesterday?" Her dad still breathed easily.

"Yes, and you'll never guess what bad news we got."

"What?"

"Well, there we are—Erin, Joann, Katie, and me, all happy, you know, putting up our posters. We just get a few up, and guess who comes along?"

"The Coronado Club." Her dad smiled.

"How did you know?" Tess looked at him in surprise. "So they have these giant posters. I don't even know how they got them made. But when they taped them up, ours looked like postage stamps. Then I read the poster, and you'll never guess what it says."

"You're right; I'll never guess. So tell me." Dad pointed to a turn in the trail. "Watch out; we don't want another fall. It gets steep and rocky here."

Looking ahead and noting the turn, Tess corrected her steps and kept talking. "So I'm reading this poster, and it says, 'If we win, we will buy the whole sixth grade pizza on the day we paint the mural.' The whole sixth grade! Lauren's dad is going to pay. Can you believe it?"

"I hope you don't think I'm going to match that offer," her dad said.

"Of course not. It's a bribe!"

"Yes, it is. I thought Lauren was running for Miss Coronado. That's one reason you dropped out, right? So she could win and you guys would win the mural?"

"Well, that's what I thought, too. But yesterday she said she was dropping out so Melody could win Miss Coronado and she could win the mural with Colleen. She said she wouldn't pass up the chance to paint with her 'best bud.'" Tess spat the words out.

Colleen had backstabbed Tess for Lauren in the beginning of the year, destroying Tess's trust and any friendly feelings she had toward Colleen.

"You know what it sounds like to me?" her dad asked.

"What?" Tess said. For once Dad couldn't say anything goody gumdrop about the situation.

"It sounds as if Lauren is a lot like you."

He had to be kidding. "Dad! How can you say that? She's a total snob and rude and everything." Tess stopped. She ground her toe into the dew-damp trail and looked her father square in the eye.

"Now, now, I didn't mean in every way." Her father checked his watch. "You're much nicer than she is, I'm sure. And I know how much she hurt you. You had a right to be upset about that. I only meant that you dropped out of the Miss Coronado race for Erin's sake, and Lauren did for her best friend, too. Maybe they're not so different from you."

"No way. Lauren just wants fame, and the wall lasts longer. They want the Coronado Club to win everything. Lauren even said so. And besides, I did drop out for Erin but also because I read a Bible verse and I thought God wanted me to." Keeping her eyes on the trail, she marched forward, heart thumping. It wasn't just from the exercise. Her father was lukewarm on Christianity, and she didn't know how he would take her saying she thought God had told her something.

"Oh yeah, what was that?" Her dad waved toward the steep incline that lay before them.

"It-it was about honoring your brother and sister more than yourself."

"I see." Her dad was silent a minute. Tess glanced at a Claretcup Cholla cactus. Tiny red buds were closed tight as clenched fists at the end of their long-armed stems. In another month they would unfold to catch the sun's mid-March rays.

"Well, if that's what you're learning at church, I'm all for it. Let's see if you can honor your brother at home, too."

Dad was in such a good mood she might as well ask about Tyler. "Actually, I was hoping you would let Tyler come to church with me. I mean, that would be a good way to honor him, right? By including him?" Tess talked fast, anxiety coursing through her body.

"Did you ask him already?" Her dad's voice had a sharp, you're-in-trouble edge.

"Not really." Tess gulped. "I told him I'd ask Josh if there were parties for his age. But I didn't even do that yet. I wanted to ask you first."

"Oh." The muscles on his neck relaxed a bit. "I don't know." Mr. Thomas took off his cap and rubbed his forehead, a sure sign of distress. Uh-oh. Had she asked too soon?

"I'll think about it," he said. "Now, let's get this last part over with so we can enjoy the view." They finished the last bit of the trail, sometimes using both hands and feet, to reach their reward at the top. From the perch they could see the morning poured out full strength, and after a minute to catch her breath, Tess uncapped her water bottle. The cool liquid tumbled down her throat. She recapped it and stared down at the Valley of the Sun.

Swatches of green grass blended with patches of gray gravel. Spring was about to arrive. The blooms waited impatiently to come out.

"Is this what it feels like to be on top of the world?" she wondered aloud.

"I think so, Tess, I think so."

Five minutes later he touched her shoulder and motioned toward the trail. "I think we should head back."

When she got home from hiking, it was still too early to call Erin to find out if Tom had said anything about the secret valentine. So she showered and slipped on some sweats, then sat down at her desk to start her homework. After an unfruitful minute staring at her math book, she logged in to her computer prayer diary.

Dear Lord,

I'm sorry I haven't written for a few days, but I know you're with me and see what's going on. My dad thinks I'm like Lauren, but I don't think I am. I'm confused. I dropped out of the Miss Coronado race so we could win, but now I don't think we will. I hope I didn't waste my shot in the race for nothing.

Then, I thought it would be a good idea to ask Tyler to church, but now I'm not sure. I'm glad you're not ever confused.

Love, Tess

twelve

Golden Rulers

Sunday Night, February 16

Tess threw one outfit after another on her bed. The overalls had a rip. A bleach streak washed out a section of her black jeans. The skirt was too short—dork mode. Finally settling on a pair of blue jeans with rolled cuffs and an ASU sweatshirt, she looked into the mirror. A dot of Cherry Pie lip gloss, and she would be ready.

"Mom, are you driving me or is Dad?" She walked down the hall toward the front door. As she slipped her feet into her clogs, her mother appeared.

"Me, I guess. Dad isn't back from picking up chicken at El Pollo Asado. Are you sure you don't want to wait and eat with us first?" Mrs. Thomas pulled a sweater over her bulging belly before slipping into her loafers.

"I'm not hungry. Besides, they'll have snacks at the party." Tess glanced at her watch. "I don't want to be late. Let's go."

"All right, all right."

Tess opened the door and led the way into the star-spangled evening, the air crisp as an autumn apple. Her stomach twisted a bit. She would be walking in all by herself, since Erin and Tom were coming late. She hoped Melissa would be there.

Streetlights lit up the city as the miles rolled by on the way to Living Water Community Church. "Here we are," Mrs. Thomas announced. As if Tess didn't know.

Quickly glancing around to make sure no one was looking, she kissed her mother's cheek and hopped out of the car. "Thanks for the ride."

"Mrs. Janssen will bring you home?"

"Erin said she would."

"Okay then, have a good time."

Tess waved and walked into the church, hoping she would do just that. She strolled through the entryway and into the auditorium.

"Here you go." An eighth-grade girl slapped a gold spray-painted ruler into Tess's palm. It stung.

"Thanks." Tess flipped over the ruler. "What's this number on the back?"

"For the door prizes," the girl said, then motioned Tess forward so the person behind her could get a ruler.

Well, now what? Tess could sit here and pick at her hangnails, which she usually did when she felt out of place. But this was her church now, and she might as well get involved. Tess gulped down a lump of fear and headed toward the snack tables.

Okay! Here we go. She spotted Melissa and Terri, who were pouring sodas for themselves. Their backs were turned to her, but Tess recognized Melissa's bright red hair from the back. Tess's ruler slipped from her hand, and as she bent to grab it, she caught a bit of what Terri said.

"Well, I don't want her to come. It'll mess up the pairs.

We already have four people, and we're not supposed to have more."

What were they talking about? Tess picked up her ruler and was about to interject a friendly "hello" when Melissa, back still turned, answered Terri.

"Well, she didn't know. And she really likes to baby-sit. She works with me in the nursery, so I know she would like the course."

"Then she can take it next month," Terri snapped. "And just because you two are buddy-buddy in the nursery doesn't mean my mom has to squeeze her into the class."

"Sorry," Melissa said. "I know. I just thought it would be nice if we could fit her in. But if we can't, it's nothing for us to get in a fight over."

They're talking about me! Tess realized. And the baby-sitting course. Terri wants me out!

"You're right," Terri soothed. "So you'll tell her?"

"Yeah, tonight," Melissa answered. "So should we find a seat?" Before they could turn around, Tess ducked over to another table, out of their line of view.

Heat flushed her face. Blood pumped to her head, and her eyes felt as if they were squeezing out of her skull. How embarrassing! Just when she thought things were going better, she felt like an outsider at her own church. Would Tyler feel like this, too, if she invited him?

She should never have come tonight. If she had a ride home, she would leave right now. She should never have even asked to go to that dumb baby-sitting class.

Steadying a little pile of pretzels coddled in her napkin, she sat down in the back.

"What do you think the door prizes are?" A voice came from beside her.

"Uh, excuse me?" Tess hadn't noticed the girl sitting down.

"Isn't that what the numbers are for? Door prizes?" the girl asked.

Tess studied her face, hoping she hadn't already met this girl and forgotten her name. "I guess so." Tess wriggled out a smile. "My name is Tess."

"I'm Kristy. We're new here. In fact, this is my first week." Kristy's short brown bob of tumbly curls shook when she talked.

Tess's muscles relaxed. She was an old-timer compared to this girl. "I'm glad you came," Tess said, pleased to warmly welcome someone to the church. "Did you just move here?"

"Yes," Kristy said. "I'm from Oregon."

Tess looked toward the door, saw Erin and Tom, and waved to her friend.

"That's my friend Erin. She's been going here a long time," Tess said. Tom didn't look her in the eye. Oh no. What if he guessed the valentine was from her and was so disgusted he never wanted to look at her again? How would she handle riding home with them?

"Hi, Tess." Erin sat down.

"Hi. This is Kristy. She's new here."

"Nice to meet you." Erin smiled. She asked Kristy the usual questions, whether she had brothers and sisters, where she went to school, where she had moved from.

"Uh, would you guys excuse me? I just saw another girl from my school, and I didn't even know she went to this church. I want to catch her at the snack table."

"Go ahead," Tess said. As soon as Kristy left, Tess whispered to Erin, "Did he get it?"

"He must have. My mom said there was something for him in the mailbox Friday. She didn't say anything until today, and I didn't want to ask or they would have known I was involved."

"Does he know it's from me?"

"I don't think so. He would have said something to me. And he didn't." Erin patted Tess's knee. "Don't worry."

Tess breathed out a slow breath. At least one thing went right tonight.

The evening passed quickly, and it was almost time to leave before Tess had a chance to tell Erin about overhearing Terri talking to Melissa.

"Maybe it wasn't as bad as it sounded," Erin said. "Melissa likes you."

"Maybe," Tess said. She lowered her voice since Pastor Jack was drawing the door prizes. "She really hurt me. I don't think she would like someone to leave her out." Tess looked up and sucked in her breath. Melissa stood right next to her and must have heard every word she said.

"Tess, can I talk with you?" Melissa asked.

thirteen

Prizes

Sunday Night, February 16

"Okay." Tess looked at Erin. "I'll meet you at the car in a minute, okay?" Erin nodded and left the room.

"I don't know how to say this," Melissa began.

"I already know. Terri doesn't want me in the baby-sitting class." The words froze in her mouth, but she managed to get them out anyway.

"How did you know?"

"I was coming up to say hi to you guys when I heard you talking." There. She felt better telling the truth.

"I'm sorry. I really wanted you to be there. But Terri is right; there are only supposed to be four people in the class so we have time to do the mouth-to-mouth resuscitation on the pretend baby."

"I didn't get the idea that was the only reason Terri wanted me out," Tess said. Why was she saying this? It wasn't Melissa's fault.

"I think she's jealous that we spend time together. She's still my best friend, you know what I mean?"

Tess did know what she meant. She remembered how

worried Erin was last month, thinking maybe Melissa and Tess might become best friends. But Tess would never trade her Secret Sister for anyone. Of course, Erin was thinking of flying to Seattle over the summer to visit her old best friend, Jessica Blessing, which made Tess feel weird.

"I know what you mean." Warmer words sprang to mind now. "Will you give me Terri's phone number so I can call her mom and sign up for next month?"

"Of course!" Relief brightened Melissa's face. "I'll give it to you when we work nursery together, okay?"

"Okay." Tess said good-bye. On the way out to the Suburban, her tummy was aflutter. Tom hadn't said anything to her all night. What if he had guessed the valentine was from her? And thought she was dumb? She nervously approached the car.

"I hope you guys weren't waiting long," she said. Everyone was already seat-belted in, and the engine was running.

"No no," Erin's mother said. "I left the engine running so the car would stay warm. Did you guys have a nice time?"

"I guess so," Tom said. "The speaker was pretty good, and we had a tricycle relay." He laughed a little. "But nobody I know won a door prize. They had a cordless phone I wanted. Some dumb seventh grader got it." He tossed his head, his blond hair landing perfectly, and smiled. "Hey, Tess, I haven't seen you hiking Squaw Peak lately. You didn't give up, did you?"

He talked to her! He must not know the valentine was from her. Or else it didn't freak him out. Joy and relief filled her soul.

"I'm still hiking. I did Camelback Mountain last week," she said, a hint of pride in her voice. "But we might do

Squaw Peak this week," she said, wondering why she said it even as the words came out of her mouth. She was still afraid of twisting her ankle there.

"Cool. I'm going; so I'll look for you. We go about ten o'clock."

Erin nudged her friend as if to say, "See, I told you it was okay."

Tess smiled back. She had to convince her dad to hike Squaw Peak at ten o'clock next Saturday! He had mentioned hiking the Dreamy Draw. Who cared about sprained ankles anyway? And who needs cordless phones? Tom had talked with her; that was a much better prize.

fourteen

The Vote

Wednesday, February 19

The early days of the week passed quickly. Once Wednesday arrived, the hours dragged. Tess doodled in class, smoothed on Hawaiian Punch lip gloss, and generally wasted time.

Just before it was time for the assembly to vote for Mr. and Miss Coronado and the mural team, Erin passed a note to Tess and pointed at the large-faced clock above the classroom door. "Ten minutes to go."

"I'm nervous, are you?" Tess wrote back.

A few minutes later Ms. Martinez snapped shut her book and stood up. "Please grab your jackets, backpacks, and homework. You'll be dismissed directly from the assembly." She switched off the lights and herded everyone to the door.

Sixth graders didn't have to walk down the hall single file like the lower-grade kids. Most everybody joked and chattered on the way to the gym.

Tess looked at their posters on the wall and said a silent prayer. *Please, God, let us win. I know other people want to win, too. I don't know how you answer that, if different people want to win and they all pray. I don't even know if anyone else is praying to you! But Erin really wants to win, and she's my best friend. So please don't let the Coronado Club win. Or the Hoppers.*

"Hey guys, wait up." Katie and Joann caught up with Tess and Erin. "Are you guys nervous?"

"Yes! I wonder when they'll let us know the winners?" Erin twisted the thin silver ring on her finger around and around. It left a pink mark.

"Soon," Katie reassured. "Oh, man, get a load of that!"

As soon as they walked into the auditorium, they spotted huge bouquets of deep red balloons that said "Eat at Pizza Palace."

"The Coronado Club went all out, didn't they?" Tess whispered to Erin, her enthusiasm deflated.

"I know. I can't believe they got permission to do this. It seems so unfair."

Andrea, another Coronado Club member, strolled through the gym handing pizza-sauce colored balloons to anyone who wanted one. She sneaked up behind Erin and Tess and chanted under her breath, "U-G-L-Y, your team ain't got no alibi. Your idea's ugly, absolutely ugly."

Then she popped a balloon right behind them. It startled Tess, who dropped her backpack. Lip gloss and pens fell out of the front pocket, and Tess scrambled to retrieve them. Andrea laughed, then ran away.

"Talk about mean! I think they're wrong if they think they can buy the whole sixth grade." Erin helped pick up Tess's things. "They have ignored everyone for the whole year, and I don't think pizza and balloons are going to change that now." Erin's forehead crumpled into little lines, betraying her fear. "And our poster isn't ugly. Theirs is."

"I think ours is pretty. But theirs is too." Deep wrinkles furrowed Joann's brow.

"Come on, you guys. Cheer up. We'll win," Katie said.

"Right!" Erin said. "Now who has our poster?"

Whispering among themselves about who would talk and what she would say, they rehearsed a short speech they thought would do the job.

A few minutes later Principal Twiddle came onstage. "Girls and boys, girls and boys," he spoke into the microphone. Everyone looked at each other. Girls and boys?

"As you know," he continued, "today you have an important responsibility—voting for your representatives. First we'll first hear a short speech from each of the mural teams, then each of the candidates for Mr. and Miss Coronado will speak."

He motioned to Mrs. Froget. "Your class's team first please."

Two boys and two girls walked forward. "This could be trouble, " Joann whispered. "They're the only boys. What if all the boys vote for them? We could lose."

"I doubt it," Tess whispered back. "I think the boys in our class will still vote for us."

Mrs. Froget's team, The Hoppers, presented their idea of all the wildlife found in Arizona with a border made up of Frogs.

"It's too much like Cactus Cavalry," Erin whispered. "And nobody likes frogs."

"Ms. Martinez?" Principal Twiddle said.

"Go on, ladies," Ms. M. encouraged them.

Tess, Erin, Katie, and Joann made their way forward with

their poster. Just as they reached the front, Joann stumbled, nearly tripping over the wires from the sound system. Nobody laughed, but everyone stared at her. Bright red spotted her cocoa cheeks. Tess understood how hard it must be for perfect Joann to trip in front of everyone.

"See, they're already making mistakes," someone called out. Tess recognized the voice. It was Lauren. She hadn't been able to humiliate Tess, although they had tried with popping the balloon. Now they were picking on Joann. Anger rose like helium inside Tess. So rude!

Thankfully, they had already decided Erin could do the talking. Joann had offered, but since the whole thing was Erin's idea, they chose her. The girls gathered together, and Tess glanced at Joann. She imagined Joann was glad she wasn't speaking now.

"Well," Erin started, "we had the idea that everyone in the sixth grade could dip their hands in paint on the day of the painting." Erin's voice shook with nervousness. *She's speaking too softly*, Tess thought.

"We'll draw a line for the border, and everyone's hand-prints will form the border. That way," Erin smiled, "the whole sixth grade leaves a mark on the wall, not just us."

Many heads nodded; a few students clapped. Erin must have felt encouraged, because when she continued talking her voice was stronger and louder. "Then we'll paint pic-tures of important people from Arizona. Because we'll all be important people from Arizona someday, right?" She held up the poster, and got a hearty round of applause. The four girls practically ran back to their seats, flushed with excite-ment. The others really seemed to like their idea!

"Well, we have an idea we know you'll just love." The Coronado Club was up front now. Colleen explained their idea of people holding hands around a campfire with gold and silver squiggles as the border. Only one clap broke the silence; it sounded like the popped balloon.

Then Lauren stepped forward and flashed her big smile. Tess's hope faded as many admiring eyes turned toward Lauren. "And remember, pizza for the whole sixth grade the day we paint the mural!" More clapping burst out. A couple of boys, including some from Ms. M.'s class, whistled.

Tess looked around, and her heart sank like a penny in a wishing pool. She had given up the chance to be Miss Coronado for nothing! Sitting back in her seat, she looked at Erin, who was leaning forward, still hopeful. No, Tess decided, it wasn't for nothing. It was for Erin.

"I can't stand the thought of their winning," she whispered to Erin. "They always take away everything good from everyone. It's totally unfair."

"But there's nothing we can do," Erin said.

For the next five minutes the candidates for Mr. and Miss Coronado spoke. Then Principal Twiddle took the stage again. "Now we'll pass out two ballots. Blue for the mural team, orange for Mr. and Miss Coronado. Please circle your choices and place them in the ballot boxes on the way out."

Teachers' assistants passed out ballots and stubby, eraserless pencils. Tess circled her choices and folded the ballots in half. She waited for Erin to finish and got up to walk to the door. Joann and Katie followed shortly behind them.

"Well, what do you think?" Erin asked.

"I don't know. I think we have a chance," Tess said. But the clapping for the Coronado Club rang in her ears.

Katie asked, "What do you think, Joann?"

"That pizza was a big bribe." Joann pulled on her jacket. "You want my prediction? We've lost this war."

fifteen

Overheard

Wednesday Afternoon, February 19

"Hey, guys, finish up in here. I want to do my homework on the table." Tess pushed Hercules' cage across the kitchen table to make room for her books.

"I say, you're sort of pushy today, mate. I fancy we have as much right as anyone to the table. Right?" Tyler turned to Big Al, his best buddy and partner in grime.

"Righto." Big Al copied Tyler's accent. "Hey," he said, turning toward Tess. "You didn't send me a valentine. I know you meant to. It must have got lost in the mail, right?"

"Ha ha." Tess grabbed a bag of corn chips from the cupboard. It was mostly crumbs on the bottom, but a few big chips were left. She smiled at Big Al. "I'll tell you what. If God tells me to send you a valentine, I will. Otherwise, forget it." She snagged a Tupperware container of homemade salsa out of the refrigerator and a Coke. "Aren't you guys done yet?"

"Well now, she's a tad on edge because of the elections today," Tyler said.

"What elections?" Big Al asked.

"You know, the vote for who gets to paint the mural on the cafeteria wall. Lauren Mayfield promised to buy pizza for the whole sixth grade if her team won."

"Cool!" Big Al said. "Maybe I can sneak in that day and snag some." Tess rolled her eyes at him but noticed a shadow creep across his face. "Did you say Lauren Mayfield? Cole Mayfield's sister?" he asked.

"Yeah. Why?"

"Well," Big Al said, "I was in Principal Twiddle's office this afternoon, waiting for him to get back from the assembly."

Tess stifled a smile. Big Al often visited Principal Twiddle.

"So, I'm sitting there, and I see Lauren walk in with the ballot boxes. She turned her back to the counter, but I'm not a tall guy. I could see around her."

"Yeah, so?"

"Well, she grabbed a big handful of ballots out of the blue box and stuffed others in. Maybe she was stuffing the same ones in. I don't know. But it looked like she took them from her pocket."

Tess couldn't believe it. "Are you saying she stole votes out and stuffed new ones in?"

"I don't know," Big Al said. "I'm just saying what I saw."

Tess closed her books. "Thanks." She stood up. Could Lauren have really cheated? She was bad, but not that bad. Was she?

Tess went to her bedroom to pull her hair back into clips so the bangs wouldn't be in her eyes when she bent over her homework. She tried to figure out what to do. *Should I tell? What if I say something, and it's a big mistake? The Coronado Club would really kill me then.*

She would call Erin.

"Ooooh…" An eerie, ghostlike noise sounded from somewhere in her room. What was it?

"Tess…," the voice said. She flung open her closet looking for Big Al and Tyler.

"You know who this is," the voice continued. "Send Big Al a valentine. Right away. And put some money in it, too." Now the voice laughed, and she recognized her brother's voice as he laughed in the background, too.

She flung up the dust ruffle and searched under her bed. There was the speaker for the new baby monitor. The boys were talking through the base.

"Very funny," she muttered, clicking off the volume.

Now, back to calling Erin.

sixteen

Caught!

Thursday, February 20

"Have you thought of a solution yet?" Tess wrote out her note, rolled the scrap of lined paper around her pencil, and passed the pencil to Erin.

Erin unrolled it and wrote back, "I've been thinking about it every minute since you called me yesterday. I still don't know. Should we tell? It could be true." She passed the note across the narrow aisle. Just then Ms. Martinez looked up and walked over to where Tess and Erin sat. Oh no! Caught.

"Girls, I've asked you before not to pass notes when I'm talking. Give me the note please." She held out her slim, brown hand, and Erin dropped the curled paper into it.

Tess felt bad, but she was disgusted with the snickering boys, too. Like they never got into trouble. Ms. M. finished talking about insect body parts.

"Class dismissed for recess. Tess and Erin, I'd like you to stay behind." This was serious. The other kids looked up in surprise as they filed out to the playground with the teacher's assistant. Ms. M. rarely made anyone stay behind.

"I know you girls enjoy one another's company, but it's rude to carry on a conversation when someone else is talking."

"But we weren't talking," Erin pointed out.

"Talking on paper is the same as talking aloud," Ms. M. said. "Unless there is an emergency, you could wait until recess. And if there is an emergency, you need to call my attention to it."

Tess looked beyond Ms. M., staring at the chalkboard. The letters on it turned to white squiggles as she blinked back unexpected tears. This was too hard! Now she was in trouble on top of it all.

"Tess?" Ms. M.'s voice softened when she saw Tess was trying not to cry. "Is there an emergency?" The clock ticked several silent seconds.

Erin kicked Tess's foot and nodded slightly, encouraging her friend to pour out their story.

"It's not really an emergency," Tess started. Her eyes dried up, but her nose felt a little clogged. She knew tears weren't far away.

"Well, what is it? Can I help?" Ms. M.'s slender hand rested on Tess's. Tess looked into Ms. M.'s understanding eyes. She hoped Ms. M. would know what to do. She sure didn't.

"Yesterday my brother's friend saw something. I mean, he thinks he saw something, but he's not sure. But if he did, then he saw something that was wrong. But maybe there was a mistake. So I don't know what to do." Her words tumbled about uselessly, like mismatched socks in the dryer. She made no sense. That much was confirmed by the look on Ms. M.'s face.

"I'm sorry," Ms. M. said in her gentle voice. She tucked a

stray strand of wavy black hair behind one ear. "I don't understand. What did your brother's friend see?"

With Erin beside her, Tess retold the story of Big Al watching Lauren possibly stealing ballots then stuffing the box with other ballots. "I don't want to be a tattletale. Or accuse anyone of something, you know?" Tess finished.

"I understand," Ms. M. said. "But you did the right thing in telling me. Have you told anyone else?"

"Only Erin." Tess shifted her weight to her other foot. She had planned to tell Katie and Joann at recess. And maybe a few others.

"That's good. We wouldn't want to spread rumors, would we?" Ms. M. motioned them toward the door. "I'll talk with the principal after school today, and we'll handle it from there. And girls," she said as they were almost out of the room, "no more notes when I'm talking."

Once Tess and Erin got outside they purposely avoided Katie and Joann so they wouldn't have to tell them about Lauren. The conversation would come up, and they didn't want to gossip even though they were dying to tell them. So they sat by themselves on a corner of the grass.

"Want a Lemon Head?" Tess opened a box and shook out a couple of the smooth, yellow candies.

"Sure," Erin said. She popped a couple into her mouth. "So now what?"

"Well, I guess we wait for Ms. M. and Principal Twiddle to figure out what happened." Tess rolled the sweet-and-sour candy to the side of her mouth while she talked.

Erin reached out her hand, and Tess shook more candy into it. "Did you tell your mom and dad?"

"My dad worked late last night. So I didn't tell him. I did tell my mom, and she thought I should report it." Tess frowned.

"Which I guess I did. It always seems like there's trouble with the Coronado Club. I wish they'd go away."

"I know. I wish all trouble would go away." Erin sighed. "My dad is working lots of hours again. We hardly ever see him. He's gone almost every night. My mom says if he doesn't get some help at work she's going to explode." Erin's dad, a chef at a high-class resort, constantly struggled with having to work lots of hours.

"Yikes, I don't think I can picture your mom exploding," Tess said. Secretly, she was relieved. She thought her parents were the only ones who sometimes fought.

"I know," Erin said. "She's tired, too, from stocking and pulling valentine cards from all the drugstores. Hey, that reminds me, I have something for you."

Erin stood up. "It's in my locker. Wait here, and I'll get it." She ran into the school, her long hair flowing like a golden river behind her.

Tess touched her own hair, running her fingers through her shortened tresses. Maybe she shouldn't have cut it last month. But the warmth felt good on her neck, as she tilted her head forward and let the sun spill over her shoulders.

She sensed spring riding in on the breeze. It smelled warm, like when the heater is turned on for the first time in the fall. Next month the cacti would bloom, the trees would blossom; the baby birds would poke out their little heads, squeaking for worms.

"I'm back," Erin announced, plopping down on the grass beside Tess. She held a piece of folded art paper.

"What is it?" Tess asked, opening it up.

"What does it look like?"

Tess drew in her breath. A majestic drawing of Squaw Peak covered the page, from the gray walking path to the sea green saguaros. One had a gnarled crest atop it. It looked like a royal standard.

"I walk past that every week!" Tess exclaimed. "But I never see you hiking. How did you know how to draw it?"

"I didn't draw it, you goose," Erin said. "Look in the bottom corner."

Tess saw the scrawled name. Tom Janssen.

"You mean Tom drew this? And you're giving it to me?" Tess gulped.

"He wanted you to have it." Erin said. "I wouldn't get too excited though," she added. "He drew about five of them and gave them to all the guys he knows who hike Squaw Peak."

"Oh well, that's okay." It wasn't a valentine, but Tess wasn't sure she really wanted one anyway. She was glad to be included with his friends. Folding up the paper on the crease Tom had made, she decided she would put it in a folder to protect it.

"I guess we'd better go in," Tess said, as she moved over to join the line the rest of the class was forming. As they went in, Mr. Basil's class came out, and she glanced at Lauren. Lauren ignored her.

Tess's head was a beehive of worry. Had Lauren done it? And if she did, what would Lauren do if she found out who snitched?

seventeen

Dad Agrees!

Saturday, February 22

"I'm glad you wanted to come back to Squaw Peak, Tess." Her dad rounded the corner near the top of Squaw Peak on this prime early-spring morning. "I was worried you were afraid. I'm glad you suggested it!"

"Yeah," Tess said, scanning the hill for the Janssens. She looked at her watch. Ten-fifteen. Maybe they'd decided not to come.

"Whatever happened in the Miss Coronado contest?" Mr. Thomas asked.

"Well, they announced the winners yesterday," Tess huffed the last few steps to the top, walked in place, slowed her heart, caught her breath. A minute later they sat on a flat rock. "But not for the mural team. That's Monday." She didn't want to get into the whole Lauren business now, so she kept talking.

"Melody Shirowsky won. I knew she would. She's petite and cute and has 'adorable' little dimples." Tess rolled her eyes. She didn't really think they were all that adorable.

"So they announce her name, and she claps her hand

over her mouth like she's surprised, but then she's strutting all over the stage like she's Miss America or something." Tess stood up and strutted, fixing her baseball cap on her head so it perched like a crown.

"Tess," her dad laughed, "it sounds to me like you've got sour grapes."

"Dad! How can you say that?"

"Honey, don't get me wrong. But normally my number-one girl doesn't sound so bitter. One thing I learned in college chemistry: 'A bitter acid eats up its container.' Do you know what I mean?"

"Yeah, Dad." It was amazing how many lessons her dad squeezed out of college courses he took twenty years ago.

She got up and walked away from him, pretending to view the city from the heights. He was probably right. Where did all that anger come from? After all, she'd chosen not to run. She untied her jacket from around her waist and put it on, looking over the north side of the city. It bustled with parents driving carpools, midmorning golfers, and old ladies taking health walks. Breathing deeply of the pure desert air, she turned around, ready to meet her dad and head down the hill.

Someone was talking with her dad! Who was it? She moved closer. Mr. Janssen and Tom! She'd been worried they wouldn't come after all, but now she wasn't sure she even wanted to see them.

Should she go up to them? What if Tom asked her about the picture? She'd have to explain it to her father. She didn't have to decide, because her dad motioned her over.

"Hi there!" Tom smiled at her. "You said you might be here today."

Dad looked sideways at Tess.

Tess smiled and blushed. "Hi." Now what?

"We were telling your dad how much we enjoy your company on Sunday." Mr. Janssen smiled, looked relaxed. Maybe he'd gotten the day off. Tess hoped so, for Erin's sake.

"Oh, uh, thanks," Tess stammered. A few seconds passed while Mr. Janssen and Tess's dad made small talk.

"I guess we'd better head down, right?" Her dad stretched and tightened his laces. Then he held out his hand for Erin's dad to shake, which he did.

"Good to see you again, Ned."

"You too, Jim."

Tess waved at Tom, grateful he hadn't said anything about the picture. Maybe she'd thank him tomorrow.

Being very careful not to stumble on the way down, Tess picked her way through the other hikers, most of whom were still climbing up. Tiny blossoms ready to spring forth cleaved between oval prickly pears. Mmm. Tess loved prickly pear jelly. She was definitely ready for breakfast.

"It's nice of them to drive you to church each week," her dad said.

"Yeah. And I bet they wouldn't mind driving Tyler, too. If he wanted to come. And if you said okay," Tess ventured. "You and Mom could read the paper in peace while we're gone." She held her breath.

"Oh. Well, that's true. I guess Tyler can go once in a while if he wants to. Just so none of this gets in the way of school-work or family things." Tess breathed out. He actually said yes! Victory!

"Now I'm hungry," her dad said. "Let's get down this hill and stop off at Bernie's Bagels on the way home!"

Tess nodded and smiled, whistling all the way down the trail. "Thank you, Lord," she rejoiced under her breath.

❋

Later that morning, after scarfing down a poppyseed bagel slathered with cream cheese and prickly pear jelly, Tess went in to talk with Tyler.

"So, did I tell you I had a good time at the party the other night?" she started.

"I say, old girl, indeed you did. Almost makes a guy want to try out the place."

"Do you mean it?" Tess's eyes grew wide. This might be easier than she thought.

"Mean what?"

"Do you want to come to church with me?"

"Well, to the parties maybe. I don't know about church."

"I've really learned a lot of good stuff. And you don't really go into the church, you go into a Sunday school class with other kids your age. Actually, I think they split up the boys and girls in the third-grade class."

"Say now, that's a bright idea!" Tyler said. His face grew troubled, and he forgot the accent. "But I won't know anyone. And I don't even know if I want to learn about church stuff."

"You'll know Josh," Tess encouraged, naming Erin's younger brother. "And it's not really about church stuff. It's about truth and fun and how to do things. And learning about God and who he is. And—" She saved the killer detail for last. "They have snacks."

"What kind of snacks?"

"Well, one time on the way home from church Josh told us they learned a lesson about four men in a furnace. So they mixed whipping cream with orange sprinkles and stuck four cookie men in the middle. Each person got four cookies," she added.

"Oh, all right," Tyler agreed. "I'll go once. But I'm not wearing any geeky dress pants or a tie."

"You can wear jeans," Tess reassured him, then impulsively hugged him. "You'll love it. I'm so glad you're coming." She stared at her little brother, who looked worried and small and unsure. She hoped that he would come to love Jesus as she did.

"Okay, old bean. Don't get batty on me." Tyler pulled away. Tess gave him a thumbs up and ran to her room to call Erin.

"Guess what?" she burst out as soon as Erin answered. "Tyler can come to church tomorrow. Can you guys give him a ride, too?" she asked. Maybe she should have asked them first.

"Of course," Erin said. "Great! Josh will love it."

"Okay, I'd better go. I need to get my chores done before my grandma comes over this afternoon." Tess was about ready to hang up.

"Tess?"

"Yeah?"

"I didn't tell you thanks yesterday. When Melody was parading around with that crown on her head, I couldn't help but think how much better it would've been if you'd won."

"It's nothing," Tess reassured her, flooded by the knowledge that it was true! It was nothing! Her anger and sorrow had washed away like sand in a fast-moving river.

"Well, thanks anyway."

"Okay. See you in the morning!" Tess said, then hung up the phone. For once she didn't mind doing her Saturday chores and whistled as she got them done.

eighteen

Crooked Toes

Sunday, February 23

"You're going to have a good time, okay?" Tess walked close to Tyler, sensing his anxiety at the size of the church. "I was overwhelmed the first time, too. You'll have fun; you'll see."

"I know." Tyler stuffed his fists deep into his jeans pockets.

"Do you mind if I walk to his class with him?" Tess asked Erin.

"No, not at all. Josh will show you where it is. I'll save you a place." Erin turned down the next hall.

"Oh, I almost forgot!" Tess said.

"What?" Tyler looked up with alarm.

"Um, maybe it would be better if you didn't talk in your British accent," Tess said. "I mean, they might not know you're kidding."

"Say there, if these mates can't accept Scotland Yard, they don't need me."

Ugh. She shouldn't have mentioned it; he might have forgotten.

"It's okay," Josh said. "They'll think it's cool. I do." He moved faster. "Come on. We don't want to be late."

Tyler looked at his sister. His expression said, See! For the first time since they had left the house he smiled.

After she made sure he got to the right room, Tess walked to her own class.

She found Erin in the center of the very last row.

"Everything okay?" Erin asked.

"Yep, I think so. He was smiling when I left." Tess giggled with relief. "Have they started?"

"No, Sjana left the room, and Adam is in front with some pails and sponges. I wonder if they're planning a skit for the car wash." Sjana and Adam were the wild and crazy sixth-grade Sunday school teachers.

"What car wash?"

"Oh, sometimes we have a car wash as a fund-raiser. Look." Erin pointed as Sjana brought in big buckets of soapy water. The class grew quiet. What kind of wacky idea were their teachers up to now?

"Can everyone please turn to John 13?" Adam said.

Tess looked up John in her Bible's table of contents, then licked her pointer finger and turned to the right page. Everyone flipping through the pages sounded like the sudden flight of a dozen fluttering doves.

"Alyssa," Adam continued, "would you please read verse 5, and then verses 14 and 15?"

Alyssa's slightly wobbly voice piped up. "Then he poured water into a bowl and began to wash the followers' feet. He dried them with the towel that was wrapped around him."

Alyssa looked up and, receiving an encouraging nod from Adam, went to the next verses. "'I, your Lord and Teacher, have washed your feet. So you also should wash each other's feet. I did this as an example for you. So you should do as I have done for you.'"

The room was quiet, no fluttering pages, no joking around. All eyes drew to the buckets of water.

Sjana spoke. "If you read the whole passage, which you need to do this week for homework, you'll see that Jesus washed all of his disciples' feet. He even washed Judas's feet, the man he knew would betray him in just a few hours. In fact, Jesus says that we are not better than he is, and we are to do the same. Do you understand?"

A silent minute ticked by.

"You're kidding, right?" One boy just a few chairs from Tess finally spoke out. "We're washing our feet?"

"You're not washing your feet." Sjana smiled. "You're washing someone else's feet." She passed out little folded scraps of paper. "Everyone take one of these. Inside they are numbered one through thirteen with an A or a B. Girls take pink papers, boys take blue. If you get an A paper, you wash the feet of the person who has the same number as you, but with a B.

"Oh boy," Tess whispered. "Do you think we'll get to be partners?"

"I don't know." Erin giggled. "But at least we won't get boys."

"Thank heaven!" Tess said. Actually, she was so glad Tyler was in church today she was willing to do even a goofy thing like this. The papers passed through their row and she drew "6A." Erin drew "9B."

"Looks like I'm washing." Tess rolled up her sleeves.

"And I'm all washed up." Erin laughed and kicked off her shoes. She unrolled her socks and stuck them into her shoes. "Is your brother still saving this?" she asked, rolling a piece of clean white fuzz from between her toes.

"Yes." Tess laughed. "But he only saves his own."

"Please search for your partner," Sjana called out.

Tess asked the two girls sitting in the row ahead of her, but neither was 6B. Finally she went forward to Melissa.

"Hi! You aren't 6-B, are you?" Tess asked.

"No, but uh—" Melissa flushed deep red.

"What?"

"Uh, I know who 6-B is," Melissa stammered.

"Well, tell me!" Tess smiled. Her smile melted as Melissa turned and pointed. "It's Terri."

Lord, you have to be joking, Tess said to Jesus inside her head. *I mean, I've forgiven her about the baby-sitting thing and all, but shouldn't she be washing my feet? She's crabby and nothing like me. And she always has food in her braces.*

Tess pouted, walking forward to pick up a red pail of soapy water. She sensed the Lord reminding her that she should do as he had done for her. He had overlooked her sassiness, her being too busy to talk with him. He had forgiven her all that she had ever done wrong when she asked him to. Was washing Terri's feet really so much compared with all that?

"All right," she grumbled, careful not to slosh water on her pants as she headed toward Terri.

"Hi, Terri. I'm 6-A," she said.

"Oh." Terri seemed about as thrilled as Tess.

"So, do you want to sit down?" Tess asked.

"Okay." Terri rolled up her pants legs and took off her socks. She tried to hide the hole in one sock. Her big toe stuck out like a tongue from an open mouth. Tess sank her hands into the warm water and squeezed out the mini-sponge.

Terri lifted her foot, and Tess held it. All of a sudden she started to giggle and then even laughed.

"What's so funny?" Terri eyed her suspiciously.

"Your toes," Tess said. She caught the hurt expression on Terri's face. "Wait! Let me explain. I have really crooked toes. My pinky toe doesn't even look like a toe. It looks like a triangle with a nail on it. And so do yours! I always thought I was this weirdo because everyone else in my family has such nice feet."

Terri smiled. "Me, too! I mean, I don't even want to paint my toenails in case someone sees them."

"I've thought about that! It's strange, but I feel much better knowing I'm not the only person on earth with crooked toes." Tess laughed again, and Terri joined her. Over the next few minutes they talked while Tess washed Terri's feet.

"Promise not to tell anyone about my crooked toes, or I'll tickle your feet!" Tess teased.

"Only if you don't tell about mine," Terri answered, and they agreed.

Then Tess dried off her feet with a thick cotton towel.

Later that night, before she slipped between the brushed flannel sheets, Tess logged in to her computer prayer diary.

Dear Lord,

You are funny. I never thought of your having a sense of humor, but now I know it's true. I bet you laugh all the time. Were you laughing today when I washed Terri's feet? You knew I would sort of enjoy it, didn't you! And I feel much better about Terri now, especially with her crooked toes.

Thanks for letting Tyler have a good time. I should have known I could trust you with him! I mean, I can trust you with anyone, right? Please help him understand about you. And love you.

I'm really tired, Jesus, and I have a big day tomorrow at school with Lauren and all. (Can you please make sure that works out, if possible? Thanks.) I'm going to bed now. Good night.

Love, Tess

nineteen

Two Calls

Monday, February 24th

Mrs. Peterson, Joey Peterson's mom, was the Artist-in-Residence. She pushed her art cart from room to room on Mondays. Today they pieced together stained-glass collages.

"Do you think they'll announce the winner today?" Katie crowded in close to Tess, Erin, and Joann as they fitted scraps of emerald, ruby, and amethyst glass inside a pewter frame.

"Well, they're supposed to. I hope so. I'm so excited I can hardly stand it!" Erin twisted her hair up and clasped it with a clip so it wouldn't keep falling in her face as she worked. "Can you help me, Katie? My pieces look like Humpty Dumpty!"

Katie reached over, arranging Erin's pieces.

Tess, however, sat silently. She, too, was excited. But nervous. What about Lauren?

"Ready for lunch?" Erin asked after Mrs. Peterson had pushed her art cart to the next room.

"Sure." After cleaning off her desktop, Tess was ready to eat.

"Just a minute," Ms. M. said. "I'd like Joann, Katie, Erin, and Tess to stay behind for a minute." Tess ignored Scott Shearin's laugh. Probably he figured they were in trouble again.

"I have some disappointing news," Ms. M. started. Tess looked at Erin, whose face dropped like the Humpty Dumpty she'd mentioned an hour ago.

"Last week it came to our attention that Lauren Mayfield might have cheated on the mural team ballot boxes." Ms. M. didn't even look at Tess. Her chest relaxed a bit. Nobody would have to know how they found out, not even Joann and Katie.

"Last Friday afternoon Principal Twiddle questioned Miss Mayfield about it, and she admitted she had, indeed, taken some ballots from the box and replaced them with ones on which she had circled 'Coronado Club.'"

Katie gasped and Joann's eyes grew as wide as the open field next to the playground. "You're kidding!"

"I'm afraid not. Miss Mayfield will be disciplined. In fact, she was suspended from school for the day. It's my understanding that she will call all candidates for the mural team today after school. To apologize."

"Well…," Erin choked out, "then who won?"

"Principal Twiddle isn't sure. He plans to talk to you after lunch. There's no real way of knowing who might have won if the ballots hadn't been withdrawn. I'm sure he'll work out something fair."

The four girls stood silently. "Do you have any questions?" Ms. M. asked. Nobody spoke.

"Okay then, off to lunch, ladies." Ms. M. clicked her desk drawer shut, and the girls turned to walk down to the lunchroom.

"What a shock!" Joann said. "Can you believe it?"

"Unfortunately, yes," Tess said. "Don't forget, I've had plenty of experience with them. I can imagine that they'd do anything rude and wrong. Nothing is impossible." The others stared at Tess.

"Oh. Yeah," Katie stammered. She turned away from their usual table and headed for a new one. Strange.

"Joann and I brought our lunches, so we'll sit down. I'm sure we'll see you guys after lunch at the principal's office."

"Right," Tess said. Why were they acting so weird? Even Erin was quiet.

Once they loaded up their trays with a taco supreme, Mexican rice, and peaches, they sat down at their usual spot.

"Did you think Joann and Katie were acting weird?" Tess asked.

"Maybe they were surprised to hear you so bitter at Colleen and Lauren. I think you're still mad at them from last September. When they hurt and embarrassed you."

"Why would you say that?" Tess felt betrayed. Her own Secret Sister seemed to be against her.

"I know they treated you badly, but it was a long time ago. And after all, if they hadn't, we might not be Secret Sisters now. You'd be going through life without a sister!" Erin slipped some peach chunks into her mouth and waited for Tess to answer.

She didn't right away. Maybe Erin was right. They had really hurt her, and she was still holding a grudge.

"Let it go," a voice whispered inside her. In her mind, she pictured herself opening her hand and letting all that anger fly away. She pushed the thought away and clenched her fist. She wanted to be mad.

Tess bit into her taco and chewed it for a minute, then swallowed. "You're right about one thing. Now that I have you it doesn't really matter."

❋

After school, Tess perched on a stool at the breakfast bar scribbling math homework, eating Lemon Heads.

"Say, old bean, why are you sitting on the phone?" Tyler plopped himself on the stool next to Tess. Their mom was working on an ad account in her office down the hall, and Tess wanted to be the first to pick up the phone when it rang. She'd placed it just inches away.

"Well, Lauren is supposed to call and apologize today, and I want to get the phone," Tess explained.

"Apologize?" His face froze. "She doesn't know Big Al was the tattletale, does she?"

"No no, I didn't even mention his name." Tess smiled reassuringly. The phone rang. She glanced up at Tyler and shooed him away with her hand. He grumbled, but picked up his bug habitat and scooted.

"Hello?"

"Is this Tess?" Lauren's voice came over the line still as smooth as velvet, but with a frayed edge.

"Yes."

"This is Lauren Mayfield. I'm calling to say I'm sorry for ruining the votes for the mural team." She didn't sound sorry. She sounded cold.

"Yeah. Principal Twiddle worked it all out," Tess said. "Don't worry." She pictured her fist opening and the anger flying away. This time she let it, a little at a time. She actually felt sorry for Lauren.

"I heard from Andrea. Colleen won't talk to me," Lauren said. She blurted, "You know, that's why I did it, for Colleen."

"What?"

"I promised her we'd win. She wanted to paint the mural; she looked forward to it all year," Lauren said. Tess knew this was true. Colleen had told her that last summer at swim team.

"Well, you shouldn't promise things like that," Tess scolded, but lightly. She knew how much it meant that Erin painted, too.

"Now she's probably not even my best friend anymore," Lauren said.

"Why don't you call her?" Tess said.

"I don't think so." Lauren almost spat it out, but she sounded desperate and sad. "Why don't you?"

Now what was that supposed to mean? The hair on the back of Tess's neck rose. She had her own best friend and Secret Sister, after all.

"Well, I'd better go," Lauren said.

"Okay. 'Bye."

"'Bye, Tess."

Tess set the phone on the hook. Call Colleen? Why would she do that?

She chewed her eraser for a minute, trying not to bite off any rubber nubs. An idea dawned. She might call Colleen. But she'd have to call some others first.

twenty

On Guard!

Thursday Afternoon, February 27
Friday Morning, February 28

"Can I speak with Colleen?" Tess called the house of her past best friend. She hadn't dialed the number for many months. It felt strange and sad.

"Just a minute." The phone clattered on the counter, then was picked up.

"Hello?"

"This is Tess."

Silence. Finally Colleen spoke. "Congratulations." She sounded hard and unhappy. She sure wasn't making this easy on Tess.

"Thanks. I'm calling to invite you to paint the mural with Erin, Joann, Katie, and me." There. She had said it.

"What?"

"Do you want to paint the mural with us?"

"Uh, sure. Yes, I mean." Colleen's voice warmed. "Is it okay?"

"I asked the others, and they said if Principal Twiddle said we could have five, it was all right with them."

"Thanks, Tess. That's really nice. Maybe I could invite you to something, too."

"Maybe," Tess said. But inside, she thought, *No way! I have my friends, and you have yours. But I can still be kind.*

"Okay. Will you let me know what Principal Twiddle says?"

"Yes. I'll ask him first thing in the morning."

"Thanks, Tess. 'Bye." Colleen clicked off, and Tess hung up, relieved the call was over.

The next day at lunchtime Erin called out instructions to the sixth graders. "Dip your hands into one of the pans of paint and then shake them for a second so it doesn't drip all over the wall."

Tess smiled. Her friend's baseball cap was twisted backward, restraining her hair. Tess had never seen Erin be so, well, so in charge. Even Joann was taking directions from her.

"Erin, what colors should I mix first?" Colleen called out to Erin from the side of the wall.

"I guess the first five or six on the list," Erin called back happily. "Did you sketch a gavel for Sandra Day O'Connor?"

"Yes, and Katie is doing Roy Rogers right now," Colleen called back. The big west wall was slowly taking shape. First they had painted several coats of white over the mural that had already been there. Tess felt sorry for the people who had done that mural. It had probably meant a lot to them, and now it was covered up. She had said as much to Katie.

"Great artists used to use the same canvas over and over again because canvas was so expensive," Katie had said.

"Really?"

"Yes," Katie answered. "Sometimes that's how they tell if a painting is real or a forgery. They X-ray to see what the work underneath looks like. So the guys who painted this are in good company."

"Besides," Tess said, "they're in tenth grade now so they could probably care less!"

"I think it was a really nice thing you did," Joann said, "inviting Colleen to paint the mural with us."

"Oh, well yeah. It worked out all right, didn't it?" Tess said. "The Hoppers said they would rather plan the sixth-grade graduation than paint anyway. And I don't think Andrea and Nancy gave a hoot about painting the mural. They just went along to make Lauren happy. So the only one left out was Colleen."

She looked over at Colleen. "And it wasn't her fault that Lauren cheated."

"Right," Joann said. "So are you going to be all cozy with the Coronado Club now?"

"Are you joking?" Tess laughed. "I don't have much to say to them. They probably feel the same about me. But I can get along with Colleen well enough to paint the mural."

"Yeah," Joann agreed. "I'd better get back to work, or we won't get all the handprints up before the pizza gets here."

Lauren called from the side of the action. "Tess, come here!"

Tess walked over, still uneasy about talking with Lauren.

"Um, I just wanted to say thanks for inviting Colleen."

"That's okay. You had the idea, after all," Tess said. "What?"

"You said to call her."

"Oh well, that's not what I meant, but thanks." Lauren bit her lip.

"Thanks for ordering pizza," Tess said. "You didn't have to do that."

"Yes I did." Lauren looked off to the side. "My daddy said I'd embarrassed the family enough, and maybe this would help."

"Oh." Tess couldn't imagine her dad saying she had embarrassed her family. She wondered if Lauren heard that a lot. "Well, I'd better get going."

"Yeah, me too." Lauren smiled shakily and walked away.

Tess sat down on a lunch bench for a few minutes, letting the whole scene sink in. What a week! She glanced at the mural as the images that stood for famous people began to take shape. What would it mean to be a great person from Arizona? She blushed. Not that she wanted to be great or anything. Actually, her life seemed pretty great right now. Things were okay with Melissa and Terri, and things even had worked out with the Coronado Club—at least for now. And, of course, there was Erin. Tess smiled.

"Hey, boss lady, can I help?" Tess walked over to her best bud, who glowed with pleasure.

"Here's a brush. Get to work!" Erin teased, dipping her own brush into the same paint pail as Tess.

"So you want another war?" Tess held up her brush like it was a sword, just as she had when they had whitewashed Erin's grandparents' fence.

"On guard!" Erin said, and they fenced for a minute, paint splashing all over Erin's cap and Tess's T-shirt.

"Not again!" Tess groaned good-naturedly.

Erin knew what to say. Once again, just like sisters, they spoke at the same time. "I hope this washes out!" Then they dissolved into giggles.

Have More Fun!!

Visit the official website at:
www.secretsisters.com

There are lots of activities, exciting contests, and a chance for YOU to tell me what you'd like to see in future Secret Sisters books! AND—be the first to know when the next Secret Sisters book will be at your bookstore by signing up for the instant e-mail update list.

You can also find out how to order extra charms. See you there today!

Valentine Treasure Box

Your Secret Sister will love you for making her a treasure box. She can store valentines or just notes from you! Don't worry if it's not near Valentine Day. Any style of pretty wrapping paper will do.

What you need:
- A shoebox
- Valentine wrapping paper (or other pretty paper)
- Modge Podge (a special pot of glue you can buy at any craft store)
- A piece of unlined, white paper

Cut the wrapping paper into three-inch squares. When you have about ten pieces, dip the applicator from the Modge Podge into the jar, covering the applicator well. Hold a square of the wrapping paper against the shoebox, and apply the Modge Podge (glue) until the paper is completely covered and sticks to the box. Keep doing this until your box and lid are covered. Don't worry; the wet paper wraps right around the box and the corners of the lid.

After you've finished, tape the plain white paper on top of the box. Choose a Bible verse, and write it neatly on the paper. Decorate with pompoms, ribbons, and bows or whatever you like! Happy Valentine Day!

What would be awesome, just like heaven? Fill in these clues, then read Book seven!

Across

4 Playful relative of the whale
5 Not found
6 More than a twosome and less than a fivesome
9 Southern California fun town
11 Not a train or a car but a . . .
14 It's hard to do, but necessary; to comply
15 A fun, unusual, suspenseful experience
16 Theme park where dolphins and penguins play

Down

1 Away from home to visit, explore, and have fun
2 Not your father but your . . .
3 A present
7 Out-of-school vacation after New Year's
8 Horned toad classification
10 Food delivered to your hotel room is called "Room _____"
12 Shaking in your boots
13 Where you sleep on vacation